you lose these
+ other stories

About the author

Goldie Goldbloom grew up in Western Australia and is spitting mad that she has been in Chicago for the past eighteen years. She is a fat, Coca-Cola–addicted tomboy who likes to dig in the mud, read books, hang out with friends and drive on narrow roads in Italy. She writes. A lot. She has eight kids and is pretty sappy about them, but is also likely to completely trounce them all at Scrabble with little or no compunction. The woman at the local exercise class groans every time Goldie walks in because, besides introductions, Goldie hates exercise worst of anything in the world and makes rude and complainy comments the whole way through. She once found the frame of a penny farthing bicycle in her garden after digging down six feet and donated it to the local historical society, together with a tin of lead soldiers she found down there too. When she was ten, she almost fell over a waterfall and ever since, she's been fond of the idea. Goldie works as a mentor for queer and transgender youth in Chicago.

Goldie's short fiction has appeared in *StoryQuarterly, Prairie Schooner* and *Narrative,* and she is a recipient of the *Jerusalem Post* International Fiction Prize. Her stories have been translated into more than ten languages. Her first novel *The Paperbark Shoe* was published by Fremantle Press in 2009 and was winner of the US Association of Writers and Writing Programs' (AWP) Novel Award. It has been published by Picador USA under the title *Toads' Museum of Freaks and Wonders*, and has been translated into French. In 2011, *The Paperbark Shoe*, under its American title, was recipient of the Great Lakes Colleges Association (GLCA) New Writers Award.

Visit Goldie Goldbloom at www.goldiegoldbloom.com

Book club notes available from www.fremantlepress.com.au

For Lesley
who taught me what it is to be loved

Contents

And God saw that Leah was unloved …
– GENESIS 29:31

The Road to Katherine

When I was five, my father dropped me off the second floor balcony of our house in Darlington. Now, I don't want you to go thinking this is one of those fake-oh made-up stories where Satan is a guy in a turban who has a thing about chopping off ladies' heads. No mate. This is God's own truth. Bloody straight up. When Satan appears in this story, he looks a hell of a lot like my dad: a bog-standard ocker in a singlet, with his gut hanging out, and no Y-fronts under his shorts.

I've never been sure if my dad dropped me on purpose. If he said, 'You're a hell of a kid, Care,' before or after he let go of my legs. I can't tell if he was a total bastard or just a dad who'd been listening to his little girl do a dummy spit for a couple of hours too long, and I don't suppose I'll ever really know. Either way, dropping me got Mum's attention.

She came blaring out of the house, hurdled the pool and was yanking my arms and legs to see if they hurt before Dad had stopped saying, 'Why'd she do a stupid thing like that?'

'Pull your finger out,' Mum called up to him, 'she's probably broken.'

She may have said this because my two front teeth were jutting through my lower lip in a way that looked unnatural.

'Call the doc,' she yelled, beer-tasting spit spraying my face.

'Why'd she jump?' he shouted back, with the concerned look of a Saint Bernard.

'He dropped you,' she hissed at me. 'He dropped you. He dropped you. Whatever he says, remember: he dropped you.'

I used to have these wicked dreams about falling.

In one version, I'd be wearing me dad's army coat, a scratchy greygreen thing with live bullets rattling round in the pockets, and as I jumped, the coat ballooned out like an umbrella opening – phwoop – and I'd float gently down like Mary Bloody Poppins. In another version, I was a Great White, swimming in a hot blue sea, and I rocked up to take a munch outta this dirty old man with mould growing down his back, only the fella turns into the bit of backyard I buried me head in and I've got double gees, the world's worst prickers, stuck right between me teeth. But the dream I'd wake up from, ice water in me veins and the echoes of screams still bouncing round the room, was the one where Dad was yelling at me not to be a sook. He had his paws around me ankles and he was shaking me over the railing like a bit of shark bait, waggling me around so the twin streamers of snot running out me conk don't end up on his person and he's saying he'll educate me not to be afraid of heights, he doesn't want any kids of his to be bloody pansies, and right then my hand almost touches him but instead grabs the railing, and a great string of me snot splats on his leg and he gets a sick look on his face that I just see out the corner of me eye as I feel his hands opening and myself hitting the edge of the concrete balcony with the side of me head, but I'm not stopping. Oh no. Not stopping there.

You'd think watching your kid take a dive off a balcony at an early age would be the kind of thing that permanently turns a man off his drink, but it was water off a duck's back with me dad. When he didn't make it home, Mum took me down to the pub and sent me in. She herself chatted with the other wifies out on the kerb. If he was blotto, he stood me up on the bar and called for bids. 'This kid's tough as nails. Jumped off the second floor balcony and *bounced*. What'll you give me for her?' he'd say, turning me around and punching my arms. The blokes at the bar reached out and pinched me bum, squeezed me muscles and handed me half-sucked butterscotch lollies covered in fluff from their pockets. 'Slave for a day?' they asked. 'Give youse a quid.' Me dad would snatch me off the bar, complaining, 'Bloody cheapskates. Mob of larrikins. This girl's a flamin' miracle. Not a mark on her. Catholic yahoos in Rome are lookin' into it. Yer can't buy something like that for a quid.' I hated the way me dad turned me around just as he said, 'Not a mark on her,' so that the jagged scar over me lip didn't show and I hated that bar and them stained-glass windows like it was a holy place, a place where you could get your sins forgiven or at least forgotten, the bartender the priest at the altar, mixing the holy spirits, and the chiming of the pint glasses the mystery, the church bells, the transformation, God help us.

I would have settled for a dad who held my hand and skipped on the way home, clicking his heels in mid-air and singing Monty Python tunes in a voice as milky and demanding as a calf's. He did all that, but the words he sang were the names of places he loved, those tin shanties beside rivers of red dirt, giant tingle trees' warm black boles filled with duff and ants and the smell of the sky, hot silver sea boiling over on a beach hidden inside the very land itself: Dumbleyung, Kojonup, Dalwallinu, Cascade, Bungle Bungle, Butty Head, Coal Miners Bay, Thirsty Point, Tittybong, Goomalling, Wave Rock, the Houtman Abrolhos; all stuff to serenade his little girl with on the way home from the pub, unaccompanied by banjo or bagpipes or anything but the snorts of his wife and his own tapping Blunnies. I would have written him off but he was too bloody likeable.

And there came a day when Mum and Dad were having a booze-up with the relatives and they – being more than half-pissed – thought it would be educational to take us kids around Australia. Of course, my dad was big on anything educational although he hadn't learned a whole lot from the last time he thought he'd teach me something. We – the kids who needed educating – were out on the balcony in our underpants and singlets, lolling about under the mosquito nets, sweating and playing Cheat by flashlight. What *we* thought was educational was turning leeches inside out down by the creek out the back of our place, and lining them up like burnt-out grey matches on the stones that edged the water. Or pinning beetles down over bull ant nests. Cripes, you could learn a lot from the way them buggers fought to stay alive.

But the grownups thought we were stunned mullets, stupid as all get-out, and that it would take a fair bit of educating to make us solid citizens, so, bright and early they loaded up the trucks and turfed us in the back. By us, I mean me and me brothers, Fred and Bill, and me half-arsed cousins, Chaz, Baz, and Flox.

Right off, I started whingeing that I wanted breakfast and me dad came back and started laying about with his belt. It was hard not to laugh, he was that predictable. The mums went in one ute, and the dads went in the other truck and there was a mad scramble when us kids realised this, all scrambling for the ute where the mums were because they had the fizzy drinks.

Dad had rigged up a tarp from each roll bar to the tailgates of the utes, half a tent where we could sleep or talk or play cards, no worries about getting sunbit. I sat on the round dooverlackie over the tyres. I was royalty. Me brother Fred lounged against the tailgate, which was typically lacklustre of him, because the latch was stuffed and it snapped open on the bumps and a year ago he'd done a belly flop onto the bitumen. Ended up with a broken collarbone. Dad knocked him around a fair bit, called him a daggy little queen, and hauled him off to shoot twenty-eights and kangaroos, without getting Fred to say more than, 'Lotta blood in them parrots, i'nt there?' Dad fair wet himself when he found out Fred had a stamp collection. A *stamp collection*, for God's sake. Fred may as well have painted a target on hisself.

Chaz was older than me, but she was albino and had glasses and a face like a festered pickle. Baz was a boy, a point he didn't hesitate to prove, although he didn't have all that much proof at the time. Little bugger couldn't have pulled a greasy stick out of a dead dog's bum. He was a prawn. Honest. And Flox was the only living brain donor in our neck of the woods. So I was the boss cocky amongst the cousins and the best at Cheat and the best at Liar and the best at Greed and everyone had to give me all their green snakes when the mums stopped at the Billabong Roadhouse and bought us lollies. The dads stopped too but they didn't buy any lollies. They were strict beer boozers.

It was at Billabong that I started thinking it would be ace if I could get half the kids over in the back of the dads' ute, because then I could stretch out, maybe even take a kip in one of the sleeping bags and, since we'd gotten up at four, this seemed like an excellent plan. I went to me mum and whined that Flox smelled like wee and so did Fred, and Chaz was too yucky to look at, with her specs and red eyes and ghost skin, and I wanted them all out. It would be better anyway because then the mums wouldn't have to watch as many anklebiters. Her eyes lit up at that, and I knew that the dads were about to become the proud new owners of a litter of mongrel puppies. She might not have been so keen on the idea if she'd seen Dad stuffing a carton of Swan Lager down next to his seat.

So I suppose it was really me own stupid fault what happened next.

It was hot as blazes and all you could see of the educational bloody bush was an orange-red blur whipping by in the triangles at the sides of the tarp. The wind came dry and mentholated, full of bushflies and the screams of cockatoos and the feathers of the twenty-eights that'd smashed on the roo bar. A hessian bag full of water hung at the tailgate and squelched as it slopped around like me dad's own belly. We'd been told that the wind cooled the water, which was bogus – it tasted like muddy tea – and we spent a lot of time spitting it at each other through our front teeth, which was fairly amusing, and then, when there was none left, drumming on the cab window, yowling about being thirsty.

'Me tongue's stuck to the roof of me bleedin' mouf.'

'I'm as dry as a dead dingo's donger.'

But the mums didn't pull over until Baz howled, 'I gotta poo. Mum! It's coming out in me daks! Mum!'

We'd just blown past the Nanuturra Roadhouse, not stopping, mainly because of the crabs Dad had picked up there a couple of years back. Mum says they weren't the edible kind, which makes sense, that far from the ocean. So Baz got pretty stinky before we pulled in at the Nerren Nerren water tanks. The station owners still hadn't twigged that tourists and truckies regularly helped themselves to their water. This far north, water was gold, diamonds and tiger meat.

Mum chucked a roll of toilet paper under the tarp, took a

peek at the flyfest on Baz, and told us to get going. She told Baz to make sure to polish his date till it *shone.* I smacked aside the other contenders, grabbed the bum hankies and took off into the bush. It was a bloody hot day, the sky gone runny near the horizon. A goanna toasted himself over the sizzling red sand, his tongue moving slowly in and out of his mouth like a shellacked earthworm and smoke curling off his hide. Flies fell out of the sky and lay buzzing on the ground with heatstroke. I crawled under a bit of scrub and listened to the others spazzing about the lack of toilet paper. Baz, particularly, was doing a nutter. I kid you not. It was excellent, from my point of view, and I was a happy little Vegemite until I heard the utes start up.

'Oi!' I yelled, standing up, but the flippin' tank stand was in between me and the utes and they couldn't see me.

'Hang on!'

No one looked my way. Under the tarps, the ferals tumbled and screamed and threw cards at one another: the ace of clubs cartwheeled out and snagged on a grevillea. The utes skidded onto the track and a curtain of red dust rose behind them. I heard Dad's faint shout over the tin bucket clanking of the engines, 'Shut your gobs, youse lot!' The utes didn't stop.

I ran into the middle of the corrugated road, staring at the stakes that marked every half-mile in a straight line off to forever, and at the cloud that followed the utes and my family.

Every year, tourists die on this road. They'd be found a couple of miles from their cars, legs swollen from the lack of water, their pelts hanging in tattered red strips and they'd be eyeless. Parrots love eyes. We always carried extra jerry cans of water and petrol because the distance between roadhouses was just a bit more than one tank of juice could take you. There weren't any signs warning you about this all-important fact. The locals barely cracked a smile when foreigners in Range Rovers said to fill 'er up. Later, they'd mention that another one of those slack Pommies had carked it on up the road to Katherine, silly buggers, and no one would be surprised. No one would laugh, but they'd want to. By God, they'd want to.

I walked back to the tank stand and drank tinny yellow bore water straight from the tap before counting geckoes and termite castles and how many handfuls of the hot red dirt it took to cover my leg. Even though things were moving in there – slick, slick, slick – I buried my other leg, and then my belly, my bum and one arm. At least it kept the sun off. The stinky socks were blooming, so I picked one and, holding my nose, ate it. A snake essed across the road and tasted the damp earth under the tap. It was a king brown. They have huge black eyes and a splotch of black on their heads and my dad told me they are twelve times more poisonous than a cobra: if a king brown chomps your ankle, within five minutes you start vomiting green stuff, your gums turn purple and your heart explodes. Nice. The males are so crazy they'll hump she-snakes that were squished on the road days before.

The king brown looked in my direction and stuck out its tongue to taste the smell that was rolling off me. I saw a man like that once, in the Freo Markets; his tongue was split in two, and he could make each side move by itself. It gave me bad dreams. I wasn't afraid of the king brown though, because it wouldn't bother me unless I stepped on its tail, or ate its babies, or tried to bash in its head.

I thought that Mum and Dad would get to Carnarvon and figure out they'd left me back the track a-ways. Mum would say it was Dad who'd left me behind. Dad would say she was a dog's breakfast, and besides, she's the mum, the one who is supposed to count the kids and wipe their bums and such. Mum would tell the cops and Dad would tell the whole story down at the local pub while they waited for a truckie to bring me in. That's what I thought would happen.

Now, if I was telling you a made-up story, this is where the little lost princess would be rescued by the handsome sultan. But since I'm telling you God's own truth, I have to say that I was knackered and I fell asleep and while I was sleeping, a man driving a cement mixer pulled in to fill his water bottles with stolen water, and I woke up because I heard him calling, 'Is anyone here?'

Who he thought was hanging out at these godforsaken water tanks, I don't know. But deadset, that's what he was saying, so I stood up and said, 'Yeah. Me.'

'Shite, girlie. What you doing out here, all by yourself?' he said, scratching his armpits, right and left, with a sound like sandpaper on a block of wood. He was dressed like my dad – singlet, shorts and desert boots – but, unlike Dad, who was stunted and hairy, this bloke was tall and bald, much older, and his clothes didn't have things growing on them. He had two tiny gold hoops in one ear like Sinbad.

'Me mum and dad forgot me here, I reckon.'

'Bloody sods. When did that happen?'

'Lunchtime about,' I said, but I was already cheesed with him for calling Mum and Dad names.

The sun lay squashed near the edge of the sky and the man – Scurry, he was called – offered me a cold sausage with creamy grease on its side and a bite missing.

'Get that into you,' he said.

He said he'd take me to the police station and they'd get me sorted. We'd be there just after dark. He told me to get into the truck and I got in and dropped the sausage onto the seat between us. He stared at the banger for a moment.

Right in front of me, six polaroid photos of little kids were taped to the dash board. I leaned closer. One of the kids was an Abo, dark navy black, and her eyes were closed. She was pretty and I thought that, despite his white skin, Scurry must have some black blood in him. I touched the girl's eyes. A narrow glass vase was taped next to the photos, filled with donkey orchids and everlastings. They smelled like warm honey.

To be friendly, I said, 'You've got a lot of kids, mistah.'

'Yeah,' he said, picking up the sausage and eating it. 'I'm good at getting kids.'

'What are their names?'

'What?' he said. 'Geez. What do you care?'

Folding his sunnies, he gave me a look that'd fry spuds. I ran my fingers over the photos, played them as if they were piano keys. He took a loop of fishing line, sawed it between his teeth and a fountain of spit and rotting sausage spattered the windscreen. He splashed Old Spice on his tongue and under his arms.

He asked what my name was and when I told him Bugs, he said, 'Pig's arse,' and asked for my real name, which is about as bad as a name can be. When I told it to him, he laughed, pretty much the reaction I always get.

'Care?' he said. 'Your name is Care? I've got a bleedin' CARE package in me truck? Strewth. A CARE package from home. Everything a man could want in a little box.'

His CB radio crackled and I heard '... little girl left at the Nerren Nerren water tanks ...'

'That's me!' I said, sitting up. 'They're looking for me!'

'No drama,' he said and leaned over and turned off the radio.

'That's old news. I've got you now.'

He pushed a tape into the cassette player and Mick Jagger croaked something about laying my soul to waste, a song I happen to know because me cousin used to have all the Stones' records before she barbecued them in the backyard when she went on a religious kick.

When he smiled, just one corner of his mouth turned up. The inside of his lip was black. He didn't have any hair or eyebrows and his arms and legs had whopping bald patches. He only had a few eyelashes left. As he was driving, he'd pull out one of those and balance it on the top of the steering wheel. When that eyelash fell off, he got a cranky look on his face, and after a while he'd huff, and pull out another one.

'What are you staring at?' he said, looking quickly into the rearview and touching the place his eyebrow might have been. 'You're not exactly Marilyn Monroe yerself.'

Which was true – me being an alabaster runt in homemade floral bloomers – but at least *I* had eyelashes. I imagined him in a blonde wig and fake titties, wearing stilettos and standing over a blower, trying to hold down his flapping skirt.

'So,' he said, 'how old are you?'

'Twelve,' I said, 'in a bit. I'm eleven and a quarter.'

'Really?' he said, sitting up straighter and squeezing his thighs together. 'Twelve's a beaut age ... my dad took me to Coober Pedy to look at the opal mines when I was twelve. The miners put quartz on the opals to make them look bigger. If the quartz is on one side, it's called a doublet, see, and if it's on both sides, it's called a triplet. We stayed in a dugout, a house that's underground, to keep cool. One bloke stuck an entire crocodile skeleton on the wall of his dugout. Hung opal rings on its claws. I nicked one. I've got it here.'

Sure enough, an opal ring strangled his pinky.

'Where's your dad now?' I asked.

He didn't answer, so I asked again, and he said, 'Dumb shit fell down one of the mine shafts and I got put in a foster home,' which was a lie if ever I heard one, to make me feel bad for him.

Just before it got dark, he stopped to siphon the python and when he came back, I saw that his fly was still half open so I said, 'Flying low,' and pointed at his zipper. He flipped me a look like a rat with a gold tooth. I told him it happens to me dad all the time – he's forgetful – and it's easy to come out of the dunny and flash the family jewels at someone's old granny, so I remind him with codes. 'Flying low' was one, and so was 'LBW' which meant 'leg before wicket', or 'XYZ' which was 'examine your zipper', or 'are you afraid of heights', which I told him I was.

'I fell off the balcony when I was five, or maybe my dad dropped me. Are you afraid of heights?'

'Shut up about me fly,' he said, and plucked out one of his eyelashes.

I pointed out that his fly was still open and he stepped down hard on the pedal that makes the engine vroom, and then he zipped up.

This was the first time I had ever ridden in the front of a truck and I liked the way you can't tell you're attached to the road. It looks like you're flying. When you walk, you can see your feet touching the ground, each step gluing you down again and again but in the truck, you couldn't see any of that.

'Have you ever been on a plane?' I asked. 'Or a flying carpet?'

'There's no such thing as flying carpets. It's a load of

codswallop,' he said, busy shaving the white stuff off his front teeth with his fingernail.

'Wrong again. I have a book at home that tells all about flying carpets. They gave it to me in hospital when I went to get me lip put back on after dad dropped me. It's called *The Arabian Nights* and it's the best book ever made. All the kids in hospital got books that day. It's s'posed to make you want to read, when you get your own book.'

'If my old man dropped me off the veranda, I'd have pulled his guts out of his eyeballs,' he said. 'Your dad's a danger to humanity.'

I thought of all the things I could say that would prove that Dad was a good dad, if a bit forgetful: his gentle brushing of my white hair; his reading my book to me every night – even when we'd had to haul him back from the pub – until him and me both knew every posh word; his dressing up in a sheepskin carseat cover on the way here, to try and rustle a sheep we saw near the road; the way he laughed, and called 'Gambol!' while kicking out his hind legs and wagging his bum as our lamb lunch ran away. But I couldn't say these things to Scurry, mostly because he wouldn't believe them, but also because it was hard to think about Dad that way ... like maybe he really was a good dad or at least trying to be. Also because I'd suddenly remembered the Stranger Danger class we'd been given in Grade One and how we weren't supposed to chat with people we didn't know, which it was definitely too late for, so I viciously said, 'Mum says Dad's an *excellent* dad.'

'Excellent candidate for the electric chair, more likely,' he said, and I decided to change the subject.

'Do you like to read?'

'I hate reading,' he said. 'Reading's for nongs. Who the hell would ever believe in a flying carpet except for a total nong?'

I touched the photo of the Abo girl with me big toe. She had her dad's nose. I thought I could see that. I wondered if she liked her dad. If she let him boss her around or if she imagined him in hot pants and a beehive hairdo.

'You know, Scurry, the way you got your belt, your belly looks like a humungous grandma bosom. I tell my dad all the time that if he keeps on drinking beer and eating snakes, he's going to get diabetes. The way you're going, that could happen to you too.'

'It's all muscle,' he said, patting his gut and giving me a dodgy look.

'Like fun,' I said, 'I can hear it sloshing.'

'That's the cement,' said he.

He had a head on him like a sucked mango. Dad's a bricklayer. I happen to know that cement hardens in ninety minutes and we'd been flying down the road to Katherine way longer than that. I closed my eyes and I could still see the photos of his six little kids, their faces floating and ghosty in that colourless forest.

'Do your kids like to read?'

'What kids?' he said.

Scurry was playing with my head; he thought that kind of thing was funny. Dad did too. I wanted to cry just then, but no. I'd taught Fred and Bill and Chaz and Baz and Flox my special method of not crying and it was this: You picture yourself as a two-by-four. Hitting doesn't hurt you; names don't hurt; forgetting doesn't hurt. Whoever's pounding on you feels it when they connect, feels the little bones in their hands snapping, splinters from you stuck so far into them that they poke out the other side. Your guts beg them to hit you again, and you smile a wooden smile when they do.

So when he said, 'What kids?' I smiled.

The truck surfed through the night sky, the flick of light on the marker stakes the only thing to say we hadn't gone roaring off through the uncharted bush, and the darkness made me itchy. Scratchy in all the wrong places. It felt like something had climbed into the cab and sat down between us. The door wasn't locked. I could have jumped, flown out into that blackness if I'd wanted to, like an apple core or a beer can. If I'd had an army coat, I might have jumped. It could have worked. The coat could have opened with a phwoop and floated me down. It's London to a brick that he didn't lock the door because he thought I wasn't game for taking a ten-foot header out into the quartzy dust, but that was nothing compared to a swan dive from a second floor balcony. He just didn't know my history.

Instead of jumping, I said, 'Do you want to hear an interesting story? I could tell you the one about Sinbad.' Which I thought would interest a bloke with earrings.

'No,' he said.

'It's in my book.'

'Listen, squid, I wouldn't be so chuffed about that bloody book if I was you. You only got it because your old man chucked you off a balcony.'

'He might not have dropped me. I might have jumped. I think I did jump.'

'*If* you jumped,' he said, 'why'd you land on your head?'

'You're yucky,' I said and I twisted and kicked him as hard as I could in the place that everyone says hurts the most, the toyshop under the awning, and it was squashy there and he screamed, 'You liddle bugger!' and grabbed my ankle, reeling me in as the truck swerved to the left and I bashed my head on something. The drying concrete squealed and metal parts I didn't know the names of ranted as the right side of the truck rose and stars spun down into the window. I thought we'd roll over. I thought we'd have mushy grey brainstuff on our faces, and broken glass for diamond rings, but Scurry didn't let the truck escape. It bumped back onto all its wheels, and the glovebox sprang open and his polaroid camera fell out in me lap. Black pearls of sweat shone on the camera, smelling of motor oil, trembling before they slid down and bled into me cotton bloomers. I put the camera back, next to the duct tape and the filleting knife, and shut the little door with a click that made Scurry flinch.

'You're a bastard,' I said, watching his face in the black reflection of the side window.

'The only bastard you know is the one who dropped their kid off a balcony,' he said, grinning like a shot fox, and the truck hit a marker. The stake flew up past my window, a comet, or a falling star, just a blur inside my eyeballs.

'They should have locked him up,' he said. 'Why didn't they?'

I didn't want to talk about my dad anymore with this mangy bloke with no eyelashes, so I stuck my fingers in my ears and said, 'Woo woo woo woo.' Another marker whipped up, hit the silver bulldog on the front of the truck and shattered.

He yanked my hand away from my ear and said, 'I bet you told them you fell.'

Which was the truth. Straight up. I lied to the doctor who

asked me how I fell, and I lied to the nurses and, what the heck, I lied to Scurry too. I'm the queen of Liar. But I put me fingers back in me ears and closed me eyes and whispered 'Woo woo' like it was a spell, some kind of voodoo prayer that could turn me into someone else. After listening to me for a while, he cranked up old Mick, and lay another eyelash on the steering wheel.

'Scurry,' I said, 'I could tell you a different story. Something you'll like.'

He didn't say anything for a long time.

'I could tell you about Scheherazade. She's the towelhead who told all the stories in me book, a thousand and one stories, one every night.'

'Why?' he asked, glancing at me and his eyes looked huge and black. He bunged on the brakes and pulled off the road. I didn't have the foggiest where we were. Somewhere dark, in the back of beyond. He opened his door and told me to get out. The wind from the coast was strong enough to blow a dog off its chain and it thudded in my ears, blew the hairs in me eyebrows backwards, whipped me eyelashes against my dry eyeballs. I could barely suck in a breath, the air rushed by so fast. A sheet of sand peeled off and snapped a few feet from the ground. My shorts rippled, my shirt ballooned, hair lashed my face. I felt my body lifting, my feet barely touching the ground.

At last, he asked, 'Why did she tell so many of them stories?'

He held my wrist so I wouldn't blow away. I could smell his strong penicillin smell and the Old Spice on his tongue. The polaroid camera, shoved by the wind, hit me, and it smelled like a gun after it goes off. He put his sunnies on.

'Just listen,' I said. 'There was once a wicked king, who got married to a different girl every night, and every morning, he'd cut off her head.'

'Hah!' he laughed, '*Excellent.*'

'I told you you'd like it. It's your kind of story. Scheherazade offered to get married to him. All the other girls was forced, but she offered. She told her sister to come in the night, and then she told her a story, and the shah began to listen too, because she was a dinkum storyteller. Right when the sun come up, she stopped. She wouldn't tell the end.'

'Did he kill her?' he asked and I smelled the old fish stink of the knife.

'No. The shah wanted to hear the end of the story, so he let her live and she come to him the next night, and that night, she done the same thing. Told a story, but not the end.'

'For a thousand and one nights.'

'Yeah. And he let her live because he liked her stories.'

His voice floated to me, soft in the darkness. 'They must have been good stories.'

'I could tell you a good story,' I said.

'Go on then,' he said. 'Tell me.'

The wind shouting through the casuarinas, the strips of hanging bark pattering against the gum trees, the boobooking of the tawny frogmouths, everything, stilled, and the bush breathed deeply, waiting.

You Lose These: A Queer Ulysses

PART ONE: The Telemachiad

1. Telemachus

Stately, plump Brocha Feilingold came from the stairhead, bearing a ritual washing bowl in which a cup of water and a towel lay cramped. A yellow dressing gown, ungirdled, floated behind her in the mild morning air. She held the bowl aloft and intoned: *'Shtei oif, shtei oif, l'avodas haBoreh.'* (Get up, get up, to serve the Creator.) It was June 16, 1988, and a foul day in Brooklyn, New York, a day full of heat and fug and exploding bags of rotted fish heads.

Later in the morning, in an attempt to get a breath of something not already decayed, Brocha and Tzivia Davidov climbed up on the tarred roof of the dormitory at 781 Eastern Parkway and looked down at the Hassidim rushing home from synagogue.

'What's wrong with that new girl, the one from South Africa – Geo?' asked Tzivia. 'Walks around after me like a puppy.'

'She has a crush on you.'

'Girls don't have crushes on other girls.' Tzivia's face reddened. Her breath came a little uneven.

2. Nestor

Tzivia, like all the other girls in Crown Heights, worked two jobs, both in teaching. The kids were bored, the teachers were bored, the sagging ceiling tiles, for pity's sake, were bored. She eased her long sleeve up her arm to check the time. It was five minutes till the bell, but she let the little clones out and went to get her pay cheque from the bookkeeper, Mrs Queasy.

'You should really save this for your wedding,' she told Tzivia, withholding the cheque.

'I'm not engaged.'

'But you will be, God willing.'

'Who says I want to get married?' Tzivia put out her hand. She hated bearded faces. She hated the bellies and backsides on the boys who bobbled up and down Kingston Avenue. The clock ticked once. Then again.

'That's lesbo talk,' said the bookkeeper. She inflated one nostril. She could do that at will. She must have practised in front of the bathroom mirror. 'Are *you* a lesbo?'

'What does not wanting to get married right now have to do with being a ... a ...' Tzivia didn't want to say the word. Oh God oh God oh God oh God maybe she was one. Maybe Geo Bloom was one. Maybe they'd do *unspeakable things* together. She did not like the way her heart moved in the cavity of her chest when she thought of Geo Bloom doing unspeakable things with her. She slapped her hands on the desk and leaned forward, not willing to be flayed with a word. Just a word. That's all it was. A word. '... Lesbian?'

'Those are the comments that ruin your chances of ever finding a match,' said Mrs Queasy, and Tzivia's lip quivered, she shivered, she quavered, she snatched the cheque and bent her head and ran, all her fear about what life might be like without a family, without a Shabbos table, without a friend, running with her, fast and silent, before Mrs Queasy could take out her black marker and mark her for life as *one of them*.

3. Proteus

Oh God oh God oh God oh God and what is it for a woman to love a woman instead of a man? How is it that by age five you already know you may not ever cannot must not shall not will not ever forever, and why and why and why and why then do these feelings come so powerful ripping through my chest like a surgical saw with its high-pitched whine and smell of burning hair and bone this love of other women girls and Sarah Leah Faigie Mashie Sharon Chana Breina Rochel slim and graceful heads and mouths with teeth and tongues and hands and hips oh God oh God oh God oh God what will I do what can I do there is a name for this and it is me.

PART TWO: The Odyssey

4. Calypso

At 8 a.m. on June 16, 2008, Geo Bloom is making breakfast in her house on President Street. It is an ugly Victorian house, filled with mahogany and the scent of lemon oil and woodworm, and the sweat of her eight children. She walks down to the House of Glatt and buys some calf liver and a turkey leg for her husband Mendel's lunch.

'How's your love life?' asks the butcher, leering over the counter.

'Uh,' she says. 'Uh ...'

'That good?' he asks, uncharacteristically coarse for a Hassidic man. 'Unhhh,' he grunts and undulates his hips at her.

'Unnnnhhhh.' His hips move faster. 'We should all be as happy as your husband.' He scratches his blunt and bespattered chin. A roach runs across the counter and he mashes it under his thumb. He shows her the green juice on his skin. 'Roach juice,' he says.

5. Lotus Eaters

After she puts the meat in the fridge at home, she walks down Kingston Avenue to 770, the Lubavitch synagogue. On the way, she buys a roll of gefilte fish from Raskin's, steps over the urinous stream in the alley and spots her friend Faigie. From behind, Faigie's wig twitches left and right in time with her steps. Jiggle, jiggle. Geo crosses the road. Is Faigie wearing tights? No. Sheer pantihose? She hustles, trying to catch up with Faigie, her eyes on the thick blue vein in the back of Faigie's leg. But no, no no no no no no no. She looks away, slows down, looks back and then away again, and this time, when she looks back, Faigie has been sucked down the subway stairs, down down down to where all forbidden thoughts shudder and scream and blink out in darkness.

Geo steps inside the noisy hothouse homespace centre of the living Jewish world, all she's known for forty years, the house of the Rebbe, 770, sees the men tiny down below through the smoked glass, below her there, remove the Torah, covered, covered, everything in this life covered and covered always covered, hidden hiding bring it out from the aron, the closet where it is kept hidden all the time, bring it out and out and out, bring her out, oh out her out, read the words the Leviticus words, the toxic condemnation of her very essence bring the stain the blush the bright burning to her cheeks and out she goes. No. In. Not out. Never out in this place. There is no exit sign above the door. It has been vandalised or stolen, she's not sure which, the wires still hanging from the wall. She takes Union Street home, past the women's mikva, and what is that to her but a monthly descent into a pit from which she cannot rise.

6. Hades

And then she remembers, oh yes. I am supposed to go to that funeral today and, thinking this, returns to the front of 770, to the cement littered with flyers and holy words and gum wrappers and spit, where a yellow school bus awaits all the grave-goers. On the bus, she sits behind a woman whose neck is as thin and stiff as a cornstalk when winter has killed it dead as dead. She's never seen a cornstalk in winter, but this is still what she thinks. Not long now, comes the thought as she looks at the woman's neck. You'll be next. Every breath I take makes me more like you, closer to death. Every time I go to the mikva and leave my body down there in the water before I walk home, that is a death. Near death. Closer to death. Death itself. Will she notice a difference when the time comes? Or will her body, which has not been claimed by her all these years, will her body's loss not even be sensed? Thinks of running her sharp thumbnail down the stalk of the woman's neck and licking up the line of brilliant blood. Licking, licking, the fine hair, the sweetness of corn oh God oh God oh God oh God make me something else make me better cure me save me change me God. God.

7. Aeolus

OBITUARY FOR LOCAL MOTHER OF EIGHT
Geo Bloom, local Hassidic mother of eight, recently
died at the age of 44, of a heart attack, born of
excessive stress. A long-time resident of the Crown

Heights section of Brooklyn, she is the wife of Mendel Bloom, the well-known investment banker, and the daughter of Tobias Oppenheimer, formerly of South Africa, and part owner of the DeBeers conglomerate. Besides raising her family, she was fond of Italian cooking and read a lot of books. Contributions to Keren Mamosh instead of flowers please.

DEATH OF FALLEN WOMAN A RELIEF TO FAMILY AND COMMUNITY
Geo Bloom, a long-time thorn in the side of the Lubavitch community, has died of a heart attack at the age of 44. The former valedictorian of her seminary class scandalised the community when she came out as a lesbian in the wake of the 2008 court decision to legalise gay marriage in California. Her radical attempts to force the acceptance of gay people in Hassidic culture were met with intense and violent resistance and caused tremendous pain for her family. She famously lost custody of all of her eight children in a landmark custody battle with her husband, Mendel Bloom, well-known investment banker and Focus on the Family *contributor. In her final months, she lived as a bag woman under the Williamsburg Bridge and was imprisoned on numerous occasions for spray-painting passing Hassidim.*

8. Laestrygonians

Geo Bloom, forty-one, stands on the Williamsburg Bridge, dead centre. In her hand, the pamphlet with the times for lighting the Shabbos candles, in New York, New Jersey, Chicago, Weehawken for goodness sake. Are there Jews in Weehawken? Are there Jews in Rovaniemi or Reykjavík? Are there Jews in hell? Her fingers pick and pick at the pamphlet, shred it, fray it until it is a confetti that she drops between the railings and into the grip of the wind and the water far below. Takes sugar cookies from her pocket and drops them too, just to see them fall, but one is snatched by a seagull and the other one disappears before it hits the water. She removes her cheap knee-highs, rolls them into nylon grenades and hurls them out and down, unravelling as they go, coming all undone, and then she walks on into Manhattan, to a meeting she has heard of, for people like her, people who, people who, she cannot even think the words.

But when she opens the door, she sees a poster listing the ways in which people who, people who, she cannot even think the words, people can become diseased. That would be just her luck. Oh yes indeed, she has no ease. She is dis-eased. She sees the faces of her children in the close up photos of weeping sores and pubic lice and gonorrhoea, their red and squalling infant faces, she sees in the garish colours the old-time drag queens running from the Inn not far from here, chased by police and dogs and guns and canisters of gas, those queens might now be police themselves if they so wish. If they did not tell and were not asked, and wore their uniforms at work and their truest selves at night. Turncoats, she thinks, but then, what is she? Not even that. Not even that. Because she would lose everything if she wore her truest self. She would lose her home. Her children. Her job. Her family. Her community. You lose these when you say those words. And this is what you lose when you cannot say those words. You lose yourself.

She thinks of Mendel's trysts with Julia, his secretary, and wonders if perhaps he has brought dis-ease home to her from the sex object, in droplets of infected fluids, dis-ease as listed on the poster. Oh God oh God oh God oh God. How she deserves his base two-timing, craving for lusting for love, because what can she offer him but politeness? But pain? But a blank and courtly solicitude that smacks of the nineteenth century? In the face of Calvin Klein underwear men and their smooth hard bodies. In the face of string women in string bikinis. She is negligent. She is deficient. She is flawed. And so she turns away from the room where the others meet, people who people who, she cannot even say the words. She fears those big words that make her so unhappy.

9. Scylla and Charybdis

At the Levi Yitzchak Library, a basement room on Kingston, Tzivia speaks to a group of women on the difficult section of the Torah that deals with Zimri and Kosbi, the adulterous couple whose genitals the zealot Pinchas ran through with a pointed object. Could they sharpen things in those days? Wasn't there a risk of tetanus from a rusty object? Tzivia thrusts her arm to demonstrate the fatal blow and the women draw back, their mouths tight as misers' purses.

After class, Brocha Feilingold whispers to her, 'It's not the women doing men we have to worry about. It's the *women who like women* that are the real threat to the fabric of society.'

'What?' says Tzivia. 'Who?' Her face is red. Her face is always red. Like a traffic light. Don't go past here. The door to the library slams shut.

'I always knew there was something wrong with that Geo Bloom. I saw her. This morning. She crossed the road to perv at Faigie.'

'Faigie is the last person I would perv at if I wanted to perv at a woman.'

'That's the point. They're not really women.'

If Tzivia had had a scrotum, it would have tightened.

'Don't say that,' she said. 'That's ignorant. That's just insult and hatred. You're living insult and hatred. And everybody knows that that's the opposite of what's really life.'

'What?' says Brocha, her green eyes blinking, go, stop, go. The statement is slightly above her mental capacity.

'Love,' says Tzivia. 'I mean the opposite of hatred.'

10. Wandering Rocks

One in ten or so they say, and if this is true, then we shall see what we shall see. Sholem Levi Yossi Yehoshofat Yonatan, no and no and no, not them, eyes front, salute the captain of this ship, all systems go, do not abort, Rina, Miri, Lakey, Shaina, all as God intended aren't we all, oh yes, indeed, but *what have we here*? What could this mean, a broken vessel this one, true, a girl who loves other girls, not as a sister, not as a friend, but as a lover, what, pray tell me do, what is her name? Is it Sappho? No, that's Greek to us and we speak Hebrew here, or Yiddish. Tell us her name, by God, or we'll drag it out of you. What is her name? Spit it out, I say, and we'll spit her out. We'll break her of it, yes we can, we will. What's that you say? It's Geo Bloom?

11. Sirens

He has never quite understood what the problem is with Geo. How she dislikes his hand upon her skin, rejects his wettest kisses. Who do you think is handsome, he asks as an excuse to say who he thinks is beautiful, and her face goes blank and 'Oh, you of course,' she says and shudders just a little, just enough to see. 'Are you cold?' he asks and she nods yes, a play they have between them. 'Here,' he says, and covers her with his Prince Albert, his silken Shabbos coat, still smelling of the dankish wet that clings to his armpits after mikva on the busy days. And police cars wail by, fire trucks and roadkill sirens, alarms to set the teeth on edge and turn the tails of cats into banksia blossoms. 'Here,' as if what ails her can be cured by cloaking. The woman he has sex with is not his wife of twenty years. Geo's hand upon his shoulder pushes him away, but gently, and at 4:30 p.m. he returns to his office to call the other one, the one who craves his man, as his wife does not.

12. Cyclops

I'll take questions from the audience now, and what was that you said young man, you there in the back. What does the Torah say about homosexuals? Disgusting animals, debased whores and filthy trash. Animals. Say I. Lust with nothing holy in it at all and what is our generation coming to if we can issue documents of marriage to such perverts, and no, I don't think that's exactly what it says in the Torah but that is what it means. That is what it means, says I, and I am a rabbi and I know these things by osmosis. Learn some control, say I, and I'm sorry for that spit which flew out from my mouth and landed in your eye. Darn right. A liberal lie and whoever invented AIDS had the right idea in my book and a good thing I don't have television because from what I hear you can see those fruits *doing it* you know what I mean and an image like that from the sewer can ruin a child in the blink of an eye, or some chick puts her lips on some other chick's lips you can hardly call that kissing but children might get the wrong idea it's not as if your wife and her best friend don't do it all the time but that's okay because it's not as if they're animals they have control it's all about control, who has control. Abomination, is what I say. Abomination. Say I.

13. *Nausicaa*

The blacks are setting off fireworks in the streets, practice for July fourth or an excess of high spirits and love of theatre. They throw cherry bombs under the feet of 'fraidy Jews who squawk and rattle. Praise the Lord and light another one.

Three sisters watch the fireworks from their bedroom window, and Geo joins them, a younger Geo, a girl as yet unmarried, unbroken, a friend of all of them, but especially of one, especially her. More than friend. 'Hello, love,' she says, and it's permissible to say that because they are just girls talking girl nonsense. She puts her hands around her closer-than-friend's waist and that's okay too, and the edge of one of her hands, the top of her left thumb, touches Raizel's breast, and while that isn't really okay, Raizel likes to be touched that way and she leans a little into the thumb, scoots down so that now both thumbs press both breasts and neither girl is breathing. They have done this before. Raizel leans back in Geo's embrace and it is almost as if they are just friends. It is almost as if they are innocent girls. 'Don't you have to go and feed Mrs Singer?' Raizel asks one of her sisters. 'What's the time, Geo?' and it's 4:30 p.m., time to feed the senile old woman her supper of soup and soggy bread, and after her sisters leave, Raizel tilts her body back, back again into Geo's arms and Geo strokes her neck and opens the top button of her blouse. 'How is your cough?' she asks, because this is how they allow themselves to touch this way. 'Do you need me to rub your chest?' Raizel nods. Trembling in every limb. After they finish, Geo searches for her friend's, closer-than-friend's, heavy glasses. Not that they help. Raizel can't see a thing. She is legally blind. They are twenty-one and twenty and they do this thing every day for six months until they are caught by Raizel's mother, the rebbetzin, who sends her daughter to Israel and arranges a marriage between Geo and Mendel to cure the pervert of her inversion.

14. Oxen of the Sun

Geo meets Tzivia and Brocha at Beth Israel Hospital in Manhattan, all of them there to see another newborn Hassidic child. 'Cool,' she says. 'Mazal tov!' Also looking through the glass into the room full of crated baby flesh is an androgynous person. Geo looks again and thinks that his or maybe her five o'clock shadow has been applied with eyeliner. It's well done, effective. Realistic. Are you the, Geo hesitates, father? No says the person of neither gender. I am the other mother. A female then. And Geo fills with wonder at the simplicity of this arrangement, of its perfect symmetry. She swells with gratitude, with awe, with a vast love that spills wetly from her eyes. 'Mazal tov,' she says, and means it. Wants it for herself. Can taste it on her tongue like a sip of Kiddush wine. Sanctified.

15. Circe

Scene opens at Beth Rivka, a Hassidic school on Crown Street. High barred windows let a little bleary light down onto the snotgreen linoleum.

Geo Bloom has been teaching all day and has fallen asleep in a folding chair at the top of the stairs. She is twenty years old. She is dreaming.

RAIZEL'S MOTHER

How could you do this to us? I'll never be able to marry off my other children if this gets out. Such an abuse of trust.

RAIZEL'S FATHER

I hope you realise such abnormal behaviour is forbidden in the Torah. I've arranged for you to talk to the rabbi.

GEO

But I don't want to. It's too embarrassing...

RAIZEL'S FATHER

You were old enough to know what you were doing is wrong. Embarrassment is a sign that you feel shame. If you felt shame, you should have known something was wrong with what you were doing.

GEO

But I didn't feel shame when I was with Raizel. I feel shame now, at thinking of talking to the rabbi. So maybe there's something wrong with that?

RAIZEL'S MOTHER

Don't tell me any details. Disgusting.

PRINCIPAL OF BETH RIVKA

I'm sorry Geo, but I can't have you working with girls. You'll have to get work elsewhere.

GEO

I'm terminated? I've lost my job?

RAIZEL'S MOTHER

You are SO terminated young lady! You've ruined my daughter!

PRINCIPAL OF BETH RIVKA

And I've sent a letter about your little problem to your parents. They're going to pay for a psychiatrist who is skilled in fixing this kind of thing.

GEO

You told my parents?

(A dog walks by and Geo leans down to feed it.)

ALL

(pointing fingers) Unclean! Unclean!

(The scene shifts to a courtroom, where a judge sits on a high dais.)

JUDGE

Do you realise that you stand accused of destroying the world as we know it through your actions?

GEO

Uh ...

JUDGE

That you have been witnessed indulging your base animal instincts with another woman, in a flagrant violation of Jewish tradition.

GEO

Uh ...

JUDGE

And that you are hereby condemned for life. And condemned in the afterlife too.

(The scene shifts again and now Geo stands on a podium in front of a large crowd of cheering women.)

GEO

All I ever wanted to do was to start a dialogue in the religious community that might make space for diversity. I thought of it as the new Messianism. I'm simply talking about justice and acceptance for all. A kind of Jerusalem, where everyone is welcome, no matter what their orientation.

CROWD

Bloomusalem! Bloomusalem!

RADICAL FEMINIST

What nonsense. You can't be a spokesperson for gay rights. You've got eight kids, for God's sake. You're part of the ultra-repressive, global patriarchal complex of doctrinaire religious hogwash, you eat sentient beings, use plastic at the grocery store *and* you're currently married to a man.

GEO

Uh ...

(The scene shifts again and now Geo is sitting in her father's dining room.)

FATHER

I feel I must have treated you rather badly to have caused this problem in you. Our history of disagreeing. Or maybe it was Mendel? Does Mendel hit you? Did something happen to you in seminary? Listen. I'm sorry if it was anything I said that turned you off men. Was it?

GEO

Was it what?

FATHER

Something I said.

GEO

I want to die.

FATHER

Well, don't go blaming *that* on me. That's all your own mishugaas.

PART THREE: The Nostos

16. Eumaeus

Can real love exist between married folk? I suppose if the desire is there. But if it is not?

A non-magnificent specimen of womanhood she was, truly, hampered by gifts of excess weight brought on by an addiction to chocolate and a rather plain and unattractive face, of the sort usually possessed by cheese graters and the like. Her slumping, sloping inhibited shoulders suggested a little of her inherent self-hatred, not to mention her towering sense of inferiority, and additionally made it that her clothes hung in strange pleats over her deflated breasts. A fat lump of a woman, resembling most of all a large cotton ball. Dipped in chocolate. With a head scarf.

17. Ithaca

What parallel courses did Geo Bloom and Tzivia Davidov follow in their lives?

Starting both as normal children, they followed the usual paths of Hassidic girls, but then at twenty diverged, each into her own house, north and south, to bear children, produce vast quantities of artery-clogging food, balance the chequebooks, and create entire split personae which were acceptable in the environment in which they found themselves, thereby erasing or effectively masking their actual selves, in a way which is both self-destructive and shame-inducing.

Were their views on some points divergent?

Tzivia dissented clandestinely from Geo's view on the importance of exploring the psychosexual aspects of lesbian culture, about therapy, and about the viability of vegan foods as an ethical choice, while Geo dissented tacitly from Tzivia's views on queer liberalism and just how damaging living in the closet can be. Unfortunately, they had never had the opportunity of discussing these subjects with each other.

Was there one point on which their views were equal and negative? The great danger of coming out in a homophobic, fundamentalist society in which their families lived and in which they had been raised. To be openly gay, they believed, was automatically to lose everything. This, however, was not merely some delusional thought on their part, but a valid experience based on prior observations.

Did they ever come out to each other?

As certified by the guardian angel Michael, no. They did not. Although they were not entirely unaware of certain revolutionary and like-minded similarities between themselves. But even with that realisation, they were too afraid to voice the exact nature of this connection.

Their moods?

Dark.

Their hopes?

Non-existent.

Their fantasies?

Irrelevant.

18. Penelope

Yes I have wondered because she is never interested in lying with me like other women and as I am quite a handsome man slim and muscular I have suspected that there must be something wrong with her and I use the word wrong even though it is not technically politically correct or polite but she is after all my wife and I know a thing or two about Geo after all these years and it still distresses me the way she will turn her face away when I wish to kiss her but I still love her yes I do because she is the heart and soul of kindness.

yes I could have any woman that I want but I want her and she does not want me probably never has and that is hard for a man such as I to fathom and it's not the way a Jewish family is meant to work all torn up down the middle and once she put on my black hat and I thought she could have been a man but I told her to take it off because it's not permitted.

yes she told me I am so handsome I could be a model but she didn't look at me when she said it and she shivered from desire I think but maybe not it could have been something else.

yes I don't think she can be helped I don't think either of us can be helped we've tried G–d knows we've tried no one could say we haven't and if all it took was a cheque I'd write one and all would be solved forgiven forgotten and she'll wear that big hat with the roses on it once again.

yes I love her and she loves me even though she has a hard time showing it physically but she will come around or maybe the menopause will change something inside her and I'll have a wife who grabs me in the kitchen oh yes.

yes it was a good idea to send the children off to summer camp when I was busy with that woman the one who wanted needed me but it was not so good for Geo then because she missed her children and she missed the conversation with me too not the man of me but just the words of me.

yes we could always move away if someone notices something untoward and anyway Geo said she doesn't mind because she knows I need it more than her the physical part not the loving part we all need that and maybe the physical part we all need that too but she does not or maybe not from me or something else I could not say yes that is it yes that is true yes.

yes the world would be better if we were back in the olden days when men ran the world in Patriarchal Societies filled with men who really knew stuff and all emotion had been stripped from power and there were rules solid rules about what we had to do to get on in this world I mean that is what the Torah is solid rules but no one comes to hit you or imprison you if you do not do it just right and maybe it would be better if there were Torah police like the Taliban but then Geo would not agree with me there and I love that she does not agree with me I love her rosy face her good heart the challah that she bakes for Friday night yes that is why I like her love her want her need her she is good to me and understands what a woman is oh did I say that because I mean only that she is understanding of me and yes that is vital to me staying in this marriage despite Julia despite Geo's shivers yes I know what they mean yes I know what is wrong yes I love her anyway yes and she loves me yes I think that's true Yes.

Tandem Ride

I

Gneshel liked Rabbi Spitz right from the start. He reminded her of a frog. Though he was eight inches shorter than her, had a lazy eye and a metastasising bald patch, she liked him. Experience had taught her that he was unlikely to reciprocate the feeling. Orange juice and autumn leaves should taste the same, valentines and blood. She thought it was probably her frizzy hair or her missing fingers or her obscene posture that had put people off until now, but she was quietly confident that a day would come when she would be loved.

She didn't bother with mirrors and suspected that they talked to one another, passing along warnings: 'Pull yourself together, honey! Old Ugly-guts is on her way.' Gneshel struck terror into the hearts of Melbourne mothers, who quailed at her fountain pen, her scuffed men's wingtips, and the round glasses that no one considered cool. The only thing she had going for her was her diligence, which sounded a bit like deviance, but without the orgasm. If there were a department store just for her type, it would be full of nerdy, unshaved librarians.

Before she left home, Gneshel's mother sewed her five new dresses from fabric she'd pulled from boxes *her* mother had saved during the bombing of Darwin, in the '40s, and even after two weeks airing on the washing line, the cloth reeked of old fish. Her tights had thick seams running up the exact centre of her calves. She kept a ribbed leaf from Galamarrma, Darwin's Tree of Knowledge, on her bedside table. Her mother told her that it is always the girl who says no. Galamarrma was a banyan. A strangler fig. If she turned sideways, the wingtips were her widest part.

'Such a long way on the bus,' the resident advisor had said. Gneshel had been exhausted. Three days down from Darwin, across the Australian desert in the height of summer. The woman picked up her suitcase and carried it out to the little white Fiat. 'Baila,' the woman said, extending her hand, 'And this is Rabbi Spitz,' she said in the dormitory.

The rabbi looked Gneshel up and down, his gaze resting for a long moment on her face. 'You're not what I expected,' he said, and Baila laughed and said Gneshel was just a young girl, like the others.

'*Not* like the others,' Rabbi Spitz said. 'Are you?'

'What do you mean?'

His one good eye blinked.

'You're older than you look.'

She was fourteen and that very day, he asked her to come to his house and help his wife with the babies. 'Shall I bake bread?' Gneshel asked. 'Make pasties?' She had grown up on a remote farm in the Northern Territory and was a practical human being. She could knit and sew and would do so, often, for this new family. 'You're almost like an uncle,' Gneshel said to Rabbi Spitz, a couple of weeks into the school year, because he bought her ice-cream and told her jokes and didn't let her walk back to the dormitory by herself at night. 'I've never had an uncle.' She craved his pity and couldn't figure out why. 'I love your kids. It's hard to believe I'll eventually love my own kids more. I wish I lived here.'

At school, the other girls griped about favouritism; none of them had been to the principal's house even once and she worked there every day. Fraidy Spitz, the rabbi's wife, never visited the students and refused to hear stories about them. But at the dinner table, Rabbi Spitz talked about the girls over her protests, describing their foibles, their hairstyles, their hobbies and psychological makeup. 'What's the matter with you?' he asked his wife when she'd get up to leave the room.

Gneshel made lamingtons and pavlovas, thick vegetable soup with grated noodles and sliced apples that looked like swans, and brought them to Rabbi Spitz where he sat studying Torah. 'What happened to your father?' Rabbi Spitz asked. 'You never mention him.' Each evening, after she wiped down the toilet seats and laid out the children's clothing for the next day, he drove her back to the brick dormitory: an echoing art deco building donated by a millionaire after his child was strangled in the blinds. Once in a while, he brought her chocolates or lollies, as a reward for her hard work in his house, he said. She wasn't paid to help, but then again, she owed him, because she could not pay for her education. He'd taken her in as a favour to the rabbi in Darwin, who didn't like the idea of a Jewish soul rattling around a farm with a bunch of randy jackaroos and native inhabitants. Gneshel felt competent in the Spitzes' house, in the large kitchen with its good smells. She loved the red curls of the children, and the shush of Fraidy's slippers on the floorboards, and the sense that she was finally part of a real family.

Black and white marble tiles in the foyer, a mirrored wall at the end. The triple stroller crowding the crooked hallway, toys jumbled together along the skirting boards. The wife couldn't cope, Rabbi Spitz said. Fraidy sang Yiddish songs in her bedroom. Some days she didn't come out. 'Go away,' she whispered when Gneshel knocked to ask her what to do with the children. Later, she walked around without her headscarf, her short hair coarse and grey and matted. 'Here,' Gneshel said, bringing her a brush.

Gneshel sat next to Fraidy on the older woman's bed and, while she brushed her hair, told her funny stories about growing up in the bush: driving a truck since she was five, with wooden blocks on the accelerator and brake; the native children sitting on a branch together until the heaviest one climbed up and it broke under them; the underground cubby house she'd built in an old air-raid shelter; the station manager teaching her to tie tiny messages to bees, and how she'd done it once for a talent show.

Each night at supper, the little Spitz girls prattled on about their dolls' adventures. They tried to climb into their mother's lap and Gneshel was told to put them back in their seats. Rabbi Spitz encouraged each girl to eat less as fat girls have a hard time getting married. He reminded his wife how thin she had been when they first met, and warned Gneshel that men lost interest when their women became disgracefully misshapen. The body produced odd fat smells. It was only thin, lithe, youthful bodies that were attractive.

Of course, they spoke about more holy matters too: the Torah reading of the week, how best to light the Sabbath candles, why women should walk behind men and not pass things directly to them, how to get rid of chametz for the upcoming holiday of Passover. You couldn't ever learn all there was to know in Judaism, the rabbi felt, and he never lost an opportunity to educate his brood. A good question was better than a good answer. 'What living thing eats but does not excrete?' 'Which non-kosher animal produces a kosher food?' Fraidy took a jar of honey from the pantry and plopped it on the lazy susan.

'This blue one looks good on you,' Rabbi Spitz said. He was sitting on a swivel stool outside the women's dressing room at David Jones. 'Brings out the colour of your eyes.' It wasn't modest for a rabbi to notice the colour of her eyes, let alone make comments on the much-too-tight dress. The bodice squeezed Gneshel's chest. Her breath came high and fast.

No one else ever cared about her war-era fashions or commented on them. The more religious girls in the school suspected she was a hidden saint, one of the thirty-nine who hold up the world, but did not want to emulate her lack of style: the teachers suspected poverty or Prozac. A few weeks before Passover, Rabbi Spitz had told her that some kind soul had donated money specifically for Gneshel and that Fraidy would be taking her to get a new dress for the holiday. On the day of the planned trip, however, one of the Spitz children had woken up with explosive diarrhoea and Fraidy felt she needed to stay home to deal with the outcome. Later, she discovered that the child had somehow eaten an entire bottle of chocolate-flavoured laxatives, but by then, the rabbi had already volunteered to take Gneshel shopping and they'd driven off together in the little white Fiat.

'You have no idea what you look like,' he said as they browsed the racks for modest wear, and it was true. She didn't. She only had a cluster of snapshots arranged on the corkboard of her mind in a roughly Gneshel-shaped collage. He said he couldn't tell what size she should wear because her regular clothing was so loose. 'Do this,' he said, pressing his hands first against his waist and then against each thigh. After she hung up the dresses he'd picked out, he took off his long black coat and felt hat and put them on the other hook in her dressing room.

Awkwardness filled her and a suspicion that something was very wrong with modelling for the rabbi. The sleeve of his empty coat touching the sleeve of one of the new dresses made her sweat. At the same time, she was swamped with a great wave of adoration for him. For his kindness. For the way he noticed her when nobody else did. For the way, when he looked at her, his sagging cheeks inflated and sweat appeared on his bald spot.

The curtains on the fitting room weren't wide enough to reach both sides of the door. If she could see the knees of his black trousers with his fingers interlaced on top of them, wasn't it possible that he could see her homemade cotton bloomers? With one hand, Gneshel held the curtains shut and with the other, she struggled to unzip the skirt.

'Try this,' he said, pushing a hanger past the curtain. She jumped.

'It doesn't have sleeves.'

'You could wear it over something. Or put on a cardigan.'

In class, the Chief Rabbi of Sydney had told the girls that they should never buy immodest garments. Like the Satan dressed in a silken *zupitse*, these clothes were designed to seduce them away from inner restraint. First, they'd wear that clothing with a long sleeved T-shirt underneath, and the next thing you knew the girls would be stripping in a go-go bar.

She took the dress from Rabbi Spitz and shimmied into it, splaying her fingers over her bare shoulders. She felt naughty.

'Can I see?' he asked. 'Will you show me?'

'No! Don't look.' The air was cold. She hated air-conditioning. Just before peeling the dress off, she pressed her hands, as he had suggested, against the waist of the garment. When she looked at the price tag, her stomach leaped into her throat. She did not allow herself to look in the mirror.

'The sailor suit is best,' he said. It was pale blue, more feminine and much tighter than she normally wore. It had appropriate sleeves and a high neckline. 'Your first ever shop-bought dress. Lekovod Yomtov. In honour of Passover.' She could never tell her mother.

'Aren't you lucky!' said the saleswoman as she rang them up. 'Most fathers won't go shopping with their daughters.'

Gneshel froze. She wanted to sneak a peek at Rabbi Spitz's face but thought that any movement at all would cause Rabbi Spitz to deny it, and then the saleswoman would leap over the counter, frothing at the mouth, yelling about Nabakov and nymphets.

'Fashion parade!' announced Fraidy when they returned. But Gneshel wouldn't try on the dress in front of Fraidy. She was afraid that Rabbi Spitz's wife would comment on the fit, make her return it, or perhaps somehow smell the changed odour of Gneshel's sweat in the cloth and know.

At the end of every day, Rabbi Spitz waited outside the classroom for Gneshel. His car, the tiny Fiat, was hard to get into, like one of those glossy white child-sized coffins. Girls and women always rode in the back, but the seat was narrow and close to the floor and Gneshel's knees ended up well above her shoulders. It was odd to view the road from between her knees. She was used to the view from farm trucks. Rabbi Spitz folded the passenger seat forwards and she ducked under the seatbelt and swung around, using one foot as a pivot, before falling backwards onto the vinyl.

The day after they went shopping, as she pivoted, she felt something touch her ankle. Rabbi Spitz had probably dropped something and reached back right as she got into the car. Much and all as people tried to avoid touching, bodies were unreliable. Such encounters were embarrassing accidents, but also the stuff of late-night giggles with friends. If only she had friends. The Spitz children talked to her, of course, and so did Fraidy. But Gneshel prayed too long and too loud. She wasn't from an orthodox family. Their business was not jewellery or finance or groceries. It was farming. Her family members included, for goodness sake, goyim.

'Oops,' Rabbi Spitz said shyly, pulling his hand away as if he'd burnt himself on her flesh. And then, after a moment, 'It's been a long day and I'd like to unwind before dinner. Do you mind if we take a little detour?'

He wanted to unwind with *her.* He didn't want to be home with Fraidy and the children in their warren of a house. She felt like she'd swallowed a basketball. 'It's okay,' she said. 'But will the drive count towards the hours I work?'

Other girls, pretty girls back home in the Northern Territory, had boyfriends who took them driving and even the girls here, Orthodox girls who weren't allowed to go driving with boys, had fathers who took them places in their big Mercedes. She wanted to stick out her tongue at them all. She wanted to tell someone: he likes *me*.

She wondered only once, briefly, when the streetlights went on, about the propriety of riding in a car in the dark with him. She'd learned not to get into an elevator with a grown man. She would have walked up ten flights of stairs to avoid yichud with a stranger. But now, she made the excuse in her mind: Rabbi Spitz is no stranger. He's a relative. And for the first time, she thought the word *father.*

'We went to pick up a meshulach at the airport,' Rabbi Spitz lied, when Fraidy asked why they were so late for dinner. 'I thought he'd like to meet Gneshel, because he's collecting money for orphans in Israel.' Gneshel wasn't an orphan. Not really. Rabbi Spitz had, so he told Fraidy, introduced Gneshel to the meshulach as 'an orphan who I have taken under my wing' and the collector had remarked on how it was one of the biggest mitzvahs to support the weak and the lowly, to adopt Jewish orphans. Gneshel peeled the dry skin from around her fingernails and put it in her macaroni. *Tatie* was the Yiddish word for father. Her face felt like an electric fence.

'Those suicide bombers are to blame,' said Fraidy, laying the dishrag on her knees and looking at it with a puzzled expression. 'You'd never catch Jews blowing themselves up in restaurants. Such a waste of food.' She turned, opened the refrigerator and tucked the dishrag into the butter dish.

The night before Passover, after they'd wandered the house with a candle and a feather, searching for crumbs of leavened bread, Rabbi Spitz said he and the children needed haircuts. 'We won't be able to cut our hair for six weeks after the holidays,' he said, 'so we'd better get it done now.' He went into the bathroom with Fraidy and closed the door. In his personal habits, he was prudish. Gneshel wrestled the children up onto the kitchen counter. 'I don't want a haircut!' wailed the oldest, kicking and twisting, her anger setting the younger ones off like firecrackers.

'Leave me alone! You're not my mother!'

'Mummy's helping Daddy cut his own hair right now,' said Gneshel. 'Just settle down for a minute.' But the child went boneless, slipped under her arm and ran into the bathroom.

'Oh, Gneshel. While you're here, can you just get the back for me?' Rabbi Spitz held the clippers out to her. 'It's not a good time for Fraidy.'

Fraidy had looked perfectly all right during the search, but while Gneshel had been struggling with the children, she'd apparently left the bathroom and possibly even the house. 'Um,' Gneshel said.

'Come on, Gneshie,' said Rabbi Spitz, smiling. One of his eyes looked at her chest; the other one looked over her shoulder and into the mirror. 'Just follow the old cut.' The machine buzzed in his hand, mulched hair falling from its teeth. 'Hurry up.'

'Why can't Fraidy do it?' she asked. Where *was* Fraidy? And what would she think if she walked in on Gneshel cutting her husband's hair? Contact between the sexes was strictly forbidden. Being secluded in a bathroom with a man was strictly forbidden. She wasn't sure, but she suspected using nicknames was strictly forbidden.

'She forgot,' he said, blushing. 'Gneshel.' He seemed to be asking her for help, for understanding of some kind.

The religion was so mysterious and so full of rules. She was just beginning to think that it was forbidden for married women to handle clipping shears when he sighed and turned off the power. 'Go out,' he said to his child and closed the door behind her. He sighed.

'A woman can't touch her husband while she's menstruating.' He said menstruating as if he'd never before said the word aloud. 'And for seven days afterwards. Fraidy forgot that she can't help me right now.'

'Why?' she asked.

'It's the medication. It's destroying her mind,' he began, but she said, 'No. Why can't your own wife touch you?' He sputtered out some explanation about holiness and impurity, health and God and public opinion.

'Not even a hug when you are sad?' she asked.

'It's late,' he said. 'I can't go to synagogue like this. Please.'

Cutting the back of his hair. His pale tender neck. The vibration in her hand that travelled all through her body. Woman are considered impure until they go to the mikva. Fraidy goes each month but Gneshel, a girl, has never been to the ritual bath. It would be an open invitation to the Satan, to fill that empty space with filth. This constant thought: if his wife is not allowed to touch him, then why does he allow me? Why? The only girl a man may always touch, regardless of menstrual state, is his own daughter.

Every slight noise from outside the door killing her. People were excommunicated for less. She tried not to touch him with her hands. Only with the teeth of the machine. His skin, though, was warm. When she turned off the clippers and passed them back to him, his hand missed the connection and bumped into her chest.

'Thank you,' he said. 'You're going to make someone a very happy man.' His hand, his mouth, the clippers, all seemed to be moving in slow motion. The lightbulbs were all extinguished except for one, directly above his face. The room so dark. A single drop of water trembled on the lip of the faucet.

Like a child, she wanted to pluck his shiny black eyes and put them in her pocket.

'Would you like me to cut the back of your hair?' he asked.

Her mother told her that it is always the girl who says no. Ficus virens, banyan tree, strangler fig, home. This house, silent, seemed to have fallen into a coma.

After Passover, Rabbi Spitz received a letter from her mother and showed it to her. *How wonderful*, it said, *the interest you have taken in my daughter and how kind of you to allow her to stay at your home during the holidays. I believe there are lasting benefits to a friendship between a young woman and an older mentor. These days, when so many people are pointing their fingers at the clergy, it seems they have forgotten that an older man is more careful than a young boy off the streets. Thank you for filling the empty space in Geraldine's life.*

Her mother still called her by her English name, Geraldine, and Gneshel snorted when she read it. She was no longer that girl from Darwin who cut her own hair and thought deodorant was a bad-tasting novelty candy. She no longer saw Fraidy's grey hair and trembling hands. The deflated belly which had once held the children. Her eyes skipped past the older woman as if she were the fussy lace curtains in front of a view of the alps.

II

Aware that she desires some response from him, Gneshel, at forty, leans back from the empty monitor and frowns. Her email was innocuous. It was titled 'Hello.' The single paragraph started kindly, a lure to suck him into something else entirely. Surely he must have read it by now?

The study where she works is a second-floor room in her dingy Bondi terrace house. Country Swedish crossed with bargain basement and lit with brass mirrors and candles; a single chair from the seventeenth century, spine jarring and impractical, serving her need to channel Emily Dickinson. Her fingers blotched with ink leaked from her fountain pen. There are droplets across the wooden floorboards too.

Does he think it is spam, perhaps? Or has he mistaken Gneshel for some other Gneshel? She takes off her glasses and rereads the sent email. Her eyesight, recently, is failing.

She is an emaciated, blurred woman, bones as brittle as sugar cookies, no jewellery, no bust, her shoes still a pair of scuffed men's wingtips. She checks her emails obsessively, as she writes for a number of papers and edits come in at all hours. Two years ago, her husband of seven years left her for a younger, womanly woman, also leaving her the three children and a tiny weekly maintenance cheque. The house seems big without the unruly presence of the ex, and the children have begun to sound more like her: quieter, less sure. When matchmakers ask her what she's looking for in a man, she says she will never marry again, and the look on her face causes them to back away.

Her four year old plays under her feet, his shaven head bare, his yarmulke lost. He rubs her feet, asking if it feels good and he smiles when she nods. 'Take off your socks,' he says, tugging at them.

Gneshel leans back, enjoying the massage; glad she rubbed her three children with almond oil every day when they were infants. She'd seen women sitting in doorways in India, kneading the lush baby flesh of the children that lay in their laps, and the sight had inspired her nineteen year old self, convinced her that touch could be pleasant. It had been the radiant faces of the children that caught her attention. Her socks are cashmere; she loves the softness against her skin.

Her son peels off the socks and flexes her toes. She likes being manipulated by his small fingers and sits still, looking out the window to the backyard. The tree peonies are blooming, all of them, and she is reminded that she needs to prune them. The garden hasn't been tended in the two years since the divorce and it's overgrown. She doesn't mind too much. She is glad no one can see in the windows of her house or spy on her as she sits in the yard; privacy pleases her, and quiet. She used to wear a long wig and let the hair hang over her eyes.

She leans down and kisses her son on his head. The boy looks up, a sock draped on one ear. A cold draft from the window raises gooseflesh on her arms.

Her email is still there, open on her computer, which sits to one side of the window. It's only words. But there's that last sentence.

Things were done.

These words remind her of the man. His head of black hair, the lazy eye, the sparse beard, the fingers blunt as bread knives. His way of speaking without accepting responsibility or blame, his mouth, hidden behind the moustache, a slash in a side of raw beef.

'Bloody hell.'

Even as she says it, she shunts her son out the door. There is a lurch in her step, a snag in her heartbeat, she bolts the door and lays her fingers over her lips.

'Bastard,' she says. 'I sound just like you.'

The garden is messier than she remembers, rose canes tangled in the grevillea. Under the wisteria arbour, she sits playing with the buttons on her linen shirt. It's the man and all that she does not wish to allow back into her mind that has her hand so busy.

The bench is uncomfortable, the wooden slats digging into her buttocks. Soon, she's up and walking again.

There'd been a call from the chief rabbi, Rabbi Karismikov, of course there had. Telling her Rabbi Spitz had lost his job, and that had been some vindication. 'Yes, other girls have come forward,' Rabbi Karismikov had said on the phone, ten years ago now. 'He's been relieved of his position. There won't be any more trouble. The family's been told he's had a mental breakdown. Seemed best.'

Under the apple, there's a stone owl Gneshel likes, the marks of the chisel visible in the granite. She remembers his little girls, their curls and their laughter. Their love of their father. The owl is surrounded by iris she planted the last spring she was in the garden and they are just beginning to bloom: Wings over Water and Caesar's Brother. Their almost-black petals electric above the coarse rhubarb leaves. Peeking out from under the rhubarb are promiscuous violets she's never seen before.

Bending, she picks a handful of the flowers. She's told a few people, just a few, about the years she was in Rabbi Spitz's school. Details about their nightly rides, his habit of touching her ankle as she got out of the back of the two-door car. The Sydney Jews had, after several months, raised their eyebrows; the car rides a behaviour highly unusual in the Hassidic world. There had been suggestions that something unseemly was going on between them.

A magpie trills from the lemon-scented gum. Gneshel stands still, spotting him amongst the leaves. The birds are recovering at last from the ravages of her unbelled cat. She smiles at the bird, as she smiled at her son earlier, glad for the diversion.

Magpie. In her notebook, she writes that simple observation and the date. Noticing, awareness, help her to remain in the present. 'He's not a monster, you know,' Rabbi Karismikov said when she'd called him back. No. It was not Rabbi Spitz that was the monster.

Wind rushes in through the window and scatters a pile of bills Gneshel has stacked on the desk and for a moment she busies herself with collecting the papers and weighting them with a rock. It's heavy, a great chunk of Italian marble, and she drops it.

There had been black and white marble tiles in the foyer and a mirrored wall at the end; the triple stroller crowded the crooked hallway, toys jumbled together along the skirting boards. Fraidy couldn't cope, Rabbi Spitz said. Their house was more real to her than her own.

She wanted to blame him.

When he pulled her against him one day in his office and pressed his lips hard against hers, she'd been dreaming about this closer touch for weeks. There'd been something rigid pressed against her belly too. He did not kiss like the men in movies or even like the young men she'd seen kissing their girlfriends in the street. He kissed like it hurt, and it did. 'You want this,' he said. 'Don't you.' Later, he'd sat her on his lap and moved her back and forth there, in silence, with one hand over her mouth. The hand was entirely unnecessary. She'd wondered if anyone could see them through the window. The kindergarten building was no more than thirty feet away. A child, playing outside, stopped and stared in her direction. Afterwards, silently, he pushed the shulchan aruch, the Code of Jewish Law, across to her. 'Read it,' he said. 'I want you to know that what we are doing is forbidden. On pain of death.'

'But you are my father,' she said.

'No,' he said. 'I am not.'

Gneshel hid from him for days after that. She walked right past him as he waited outside her classroom. She didn't return to the Spitz's house. Towards the end of the year, Gneshel's mother became concerned. Gneshel hadn't sent her a letter in several months. *Something is wrong*, she wrote to Rabbi Spitz. *The girl I know would never do this. Is she pregnant?*

Gneshel, always quiet, rarely spoke anymore; she walked with her shoulders hunched, her eyes on the ground. She bound her chest with an ACE bandage she stole from the school nurse. She stopped wearing the clothes Rabbi Spitz had bought for her, and began, again, wearing her mother's creations, unironed.

Later, she had not wanted to get married, despite the intense community expectation that, by twenty-two, she should already have a child. She did not have friends. Young men seemed bumbling in their pursuit, unsubtle in their glances. If a matchmaker approached her in the aisles of the kosher superette, she held a box of noodles in front of her face and squinted at it, pretending to be blind. Every so often, she did not come in to her job editing a messianic children's magazine. She would take the bus out to the country and get off in some small unfamiliar town and spend the day sitting under a tree. They didn't dock her pay.

Downstairs, now, her children are fighting over the frying pan. She puts her head on her arms and tries to sleep. Screams awaken her moments later: one child has hit the other with a wooden spoon. She sends them back to the kitchen, forgetting, almost instantly, what they came to her about.

When she decided to send the letter to Rabbi Karismikov in Sydney describing what had happened, she did not mention her own part in it. Even after she heard Rabbi Spitz had been dismissed and the family had fallen on hard times, she put away all thought of how she had craved his attention. For a time at least, she had been able to throw off the memories of her own desire.

In her kitchen, the light is hazy. A light-bulb needs to be changed but she doesn't have one in the house. A pall of smoke from burning olive oil hangs just below the ceiling, the older children leaning against the counter, shoving at one another with wordless hostility. The youngest sits inside the pantry cupboard, counting out pieces of dried macaroni. What food, Gneshel frets, do the Spitzes eat now that their father has no job?

Gneshel wants to exclude herself. She was the victim, she was preyed upon, she didn't like it, she was too young to know better. She wants to be innocent. She told the story as if she were innocent and everyone had believed her. The risk of the truth being discovered is *still* part of the bond that binds him to her.

Dressing her children for school the next morning, Gneshel regrets not saying more. What she wrote was too generic, not flirtatious in the way she knows he likes. Too easy to brush off. The children fumble the buttons, tuck in their shirts. She kisses them goodbye. The youngest wipes away the dampness from his cheek. The spring air blows the smell of wet soil in through the front door. A pile of new bills flutters to the floor.

Her neighbour, a bent and thin man, walks past and raises his hand, and she, as always, turns away. She has some friends now, just a few, and they get together at a local coffee shop once a week. Occasionally, she visits one of them at home, but it leaves her feeling claustrophobic, entering other people's houses. She looks forward to the coffee shop, but casual intimacies are still entangled with memories of him. She'd give almost anything to be loved like that again.

Another neighbour passes in the street and Gneshel closes the front door, so as not to be seen. She climbs the stairs to her study, away from the morning rush of pedestrians, looking for that solitude which she finds so soothing. He still hasn't responded to her email. Perhaps she should write again? It can be accomplished even as she stares out the window at the untidy garden.

What She Saw in the Crystal Ball

She knew that there was something different about this pregnancy. A muskmelon in the ruthless sun, her face swelled, cracked open, formed pustules where the juices ran on her forehead, her nose, her chin. The Martian landscape of her belly – marked with the clear and ancient flow of amniotic fluid, silver stretch marks from all eight previous births – glowed, twisted, became alien fingers holding her together, claws around her deflated skin.

It had never felt quite like this.

She hesitated to tell the news to her husband, because of her age – forty-eight – because of his tiredness, his lack of grace and his hope that finally, finally they were done, and he could sell the old pram, the cribs, the baby clothes on eBay. She imagined his face melting, oily tears of skin dripping from his beard, and waited to tell him at some other, better time.

The midwife, deliverer of five of her eight, laughed in the face of her surprise. 'Oh, honey, don't you know how that happens yet?' And of course she did. Of course she did.

This midwife had caught her babies, one, two, three, four, five – the last of them more than six years ago – and laid them on her corduroy belly, wiped up the blood, bleached the floor. She was a tiny woman, a porotic, limping crone, appearing at intervals in the bedroom sporting dyed orange hair and T-shirts – once, a chorus line of high kicking frogs – always catching those babies as they came twisting and flailing in their slippery rush to the surface.

Now the midwife solemnly looks her over, digging her thumbs deep into her pelvis and touching the actual bone, listening for heart tones. The movements are all old, older than mankind's first birth, older than her, somehow a knowledge inherited from the very creation of the world. Throughout the examination, she looks up at the poster attached to the ceiling, a baby forming ripples in a stream of clear water, subtle overlapping blues, and she remembers helping the midwife tack it up, it must have been before baby number four. The midwife already decrepit then, but full of life, scuttling around on bent broomstick legs. Already dyeing her hair orange to amuse her patients.

It was eleven and soon she would have to pick up her six year old from preschool and her granddaughter from the babysitter. She mentions this to the midwife and gets a nod.

'See you next month, then. Don't forget the B12.'

Her husband doesn't even notice her expanding belly – it's just taking up the slack, the smocked skin left over from the other pregnancies. He absently watches her apply pimple cream and take prenatal vitamins and pops one himself when he thinks he's coming down with a cold. She forgets she hasn't told him, remembers, forgets again.

Her husband takes out her menstrual calendar and stares uncertainly at the unmarked months. 'Menopause,' he mutters, and he jumps when he sees her looking at him and stuffs the calendar back in the nightstand. It's too late to tell him without his being hurt. All this time, he would have been saying the prayers for the unborn, opening the curtains that hang in front of the Torah so that she, too, would open easily, as easily as a velvet panel in the hands of a simple man. He would feel useless.

She is sent for amniocentesis since she is past her expiry date, but at the clinic she tells the nurse that there's no point in undergoing the test as she wouldn't abort the baby even if it had frog eyes and a tail. 'Orthodox,' the nurse writes on her chart, 'refuses test due to fundamentalist beliefs.' Which isn't quite true. She could never bring herself to deliberately kill her own baby. She has seen these tadpoles at all their stages of development, she has miscarried them half-done and quarter-done and just raw begun and they always look alive to her. Childlike.

One month after another slips by, the blue waters of each day rippling around the baby, the baby a god deep within, revolving gently through its cosmos, invisible, unknown. She thinks her husband will ask if she's pregnant soon, feel the baby move between them, but when it finally happens, when the baby's leg sweeps like a wave beneath the exact spot her husband's arm is draped, he makes a face as if she passed gas, breathes through his mouth and reminds her not to eat cabbage. 'For the sake of our marriage,' he mutters into the back of her neck, patting her haunch as if she's a horse.

In the fifth month, her twenty-four year old married daughter silently hands her a brochure from Weight Watchers and she squirms, aware that she would prefer her daughter to think she is obese rather than pregnant. Again. She forces herself to smile and touch her daughter's face and say thank you. And by the seventh month, when she can no longer reach the taps behind the kitchen sink, the midwife, too, is wondering about the otherness of this pregnancy.

'It's either two babies in there or the biggest baby in the world.'

She feels light, eager, warmed by a faint echo, at last, of the joy that was hers with the first child. Her eldest daughter barely raised her belly. The pregnancy only showed in the last month and the child came early, upside down and wailing, cheesy, squashed, hideous and lovely. Her husband hadn't known what to do – the child had been born in bed at home – not planned that way at all. They'd stared at the squalling scrap, the pulsing blue cord, and the pool of gelling blood and had been speechless. Except for the child's screaming, the room had been silent. He'd said they should tie a knot in the cord, but it wasn't the Jewish custom to touch a woman after childbirth, and the twisting, snaky cord – like a loop of cancerous bowel fallen out of her – had him as close to vomiting as he'd ever been.

She'd had to ask him for a shoelace, a pair of scissors, a towel, all the while unable to stop smiling, both at his ineptitude and at the sheer thrill of having discovered the face of her child, their child, because that one was surely theirs. They had both been excited by the pregnancy, read books, gone to classes, thought of names. He had held his hand to her belly for hours, waiting to feel movement. Even as the first child lay cooling between her shaking legs, they had begun talking about the next one. Neither of them had known that each child would strip years from their lives.

At the midwife's office, her body drifts gently near the ceiling lapped by the waters of the poster baby's ocean. The midwife brings in her assistant to listen for two heartbeats and together, they bend over her belly. She sees them rear up and high-five from where she is dreaming, somewhere near the smoke detector.

'Twins!' exclaims the assistant, and for the first time, looks at her, taking in her grey hair, her crows' feet so deep they look like they've been carved. The assistant slips from the room, eyes averted. Floating, unconcerned, she listens to the quiet song of the water as it strokes her back. The babies are already crowded and their movements are slow and cautious, as if they wish to protect each other. Sometimes, she feels a stream of bubbles rising under her ribs and then she thinks of the babies as fish in a deep coral sea warmed by a beating red sun. They are the kind of fish that look like lions or flowers or angels, and they move in languorous arcs.

Three days after the examination, she feels a slight pain, as if someone has flicked an elastic band at her cervix, and within moments, a deeper, more desperate dragging that comes and goes, familiar yet unloved, a rusty plough through the fertile dirt of her guts. She lies down, reads *So Big*, waiting for the contractions to stop, but they harry her throughout the afternoon. She calls her married daughter, says she feels unwell, could arrangements be made to pick up the carpool? She finds a note from her husband under her pillow asking if something's upsetting her, and if she'll bleach his underwear, and she decides to call him.

'I'm having a miscarriage,' she says and she hears his deep indrawn breath and decides not to tell him any more.

'Should I call the midwife?' he asks and everything unsaid is in his tight voice. If the midwife is called, the child might be saved.

'No,' she says, and he breathes again.

Soon she knows that she must, at any cost, get up and use the toilet. A watermelon has grown from a tiny seed tossed carelessly into her waiting field and now it presses on her bowels, rolls perilously downhill, faster and faster. As she stands, she strains and feels the twist, the flail, softer, more muffled than with the others, and reaches down to catch her own children this time.

They are born seconds apart, both perfect, their cauls still intact. Their hair glitters and dances like falling snow inside iridescent, filmy globes that bulge as the babies move. She lays them on her warm belly, watches as the late afternoon sun is refracted through their identical crystal balls, forming rainbows on the wall beside her. She can see they are tired, they are swimming the longest distance now and, as their sacs collapse, she hears a faint cry, a dying note played by a bow not perfectly aligned with the violin.

I Have Tasted Muskrat

The Appeldorns are shovelling cow dung outside the barn on a day in late March when they see a Cortina skating up the icy hill to their farm.

'Looks like Mike's in a hurry,' says Mr Appeldorn, and he prods his wife in the butt with the pitchfork. 'Hustle up and get out there.'

'Leave off, old man, or I'll glue you on some horns and a tail while you're sleeping.'

They stab the pitchforks upright into the steaming pile of manure and walk out to the mailbox, a fibreglass cow with its tail arched over its back as a cow will do when it is about to eject a hot, liquid stream.

'Morning May. Vernon,' says Mike, their mailman of twenty-three years, winding down the window.

He hands out two letters and an economy-sized can of Bag Balm.

'I'll have that,' says Mr Appeldorn, goosing his wife aside and snagging both envelopes in a hand well-fertilised and redolent.

'Another bounced cheque. You been running up bills somewhere, May?'

'That purple one's mine,' she says, pointing.

'Don't matter none. We're the same people,' he says, taking a toothpick from between his teeth and beginning to slide it under the flap of the lilac envelope. 'You got secrets from me, old woman? Maybe this here is a late Valentine ... you sending my woman love letters, Mikey?'

'Not my type,' says Mike, looking away while still contriving to hang further out of the window.

'Give that here, buster,' says Mrs Appeldorn and yanks the envelope out of her husband's hands.

She rips it open with her thumbnail and as she removes the card, dozens of tiny rose petals fall out and sprinkle the snow like drops of blood.

'It's an invitation,' she says, 'from Gloria.'

She pictures the long-haired girl, who made everyone call her Cougar and painted her nails black before they sold black nail polish at the Walmart down to Sparta, long before there was a Walmart.

'What's that?' shouts Mr Appeldorn, twiddling the dial of his hearing aid with numb fingers.

'You old faker. You heard what I said.'

Together, they watch Mike, driving mailman-style from the passenger side of his car, speed off to surprise Avalanche, Wisconsin, with the news that Gloria Appeldorn had finally written to her poor parents after twenty-odd years out on the west coast doing God-alone-knows-what and, lo and behold, if she isn't getting married. The car fishtails as Mike takes One-Eyed Olsen's Corner too fast, a fan of snow spraying up from under the right rear tyre.

'The wedding's on April first ... the invitation must have got lost in the mail.'

'Damn silly time to get hitched. Typical of her.'

'You can get Pederson over to help out with the calves. We won't be gone long.'

'She's gotta be forty. Bit long in the tooth for that lovie dovie stuff.'

'She's your daughter.'

'Pederson's a cretin.'

Turning the envelope over, looking for a return address, she smiles at the stamp with its aqua and pink candy hearts on which 'I love you' is sweetly inscribed. She opens the card again and rereads it, wondering if the groom is anything like Mike, who she once saw holding Gloria's hand. She kneels among the rose petals and pushes her fingers deep into the snow, groping for a reply card, puzzled that there isn't one. After a minute, her husband touches her shoulder.

'Mother.'

Her knees are locked, frozen in position. If she could just put her hands together, fingers pointing piously heavenward, all Avalanche would be saying that old Mrs Appeldorn was so grateful to hear from her daughter that she'd gotten down on her knees to pray in the snow.

She looks up at her husband and his eyes are half closed, a little shiny on this cloudy day.

'Come on, old lady.'

He holds out his hand and helps her up, touching the invitation with one finger. Soggy petals stick to the knees of her woollen long johns.

A sweet champagne rises from the card to her fingers, bubbling up to tickle her lips, and she is tumbled by the desire to stroke her daughter's hair again, feel the weight and swish of it between her fingers and absorb the story of the unknown years from the strands themselves. She pauses to slip the card up underneath the layers of her parka, her sweater, her blouse, and feels its hard contours poking her breasts.

Gloria had been knitting a black silk gartel, a slinky prayer belt for her wedding, when she thought of inviting her mother. Bent over, make-upless, her mother used to spend hours each night knitting protection for her family against the Wisconsin cold: purl, plain, slip stitch over, cast on, cast off. It was one of the things they'd argued about. Wanting the orange bell-bottoms she'd seen on Lucinda Shlabaugh, the local slut, she'd nagged at her mother to take her shopping, even as her mother knitted plastic bags into bathmats, unravelling the coarse grey yarn used in servicemen's woollens, and winding it into balls.

'No one knits anymore! You're so, so ...'

She dredged for her most derogatory adjective, the one that would blast her mother over to Avalanche Dry Goods, and finally blurted out, 'Cheap!' which wasn't quite what she meant. Her father, passing, swatted her hard on the backside and said, 'Pig. Quit bothering your mother.'

But knitting was in vogue again. Now everyone was knitting – her group included lawyers and insurance agents, gay guys and – why not? – country women in loose grey cardigans that smelled like Army aftershave, all getting together to click their needles and make a little something out of nothing. And it wasn't her mother's fault exactly that she had run away. Sometimes she even caught herself singing her mother's favourite song, a song about blackbirds. She didn't know all the words.

Draping the prayer belt over the arm of her chair, she took the last invitation out of the box, addressed it to her mother, and then, as an afterthought, added her father's name as well. Knowing they wouldn't come, she tossed the return card in the trash.

But later, she is massaging herself with a Rutilated Rainbow Manifestation Crystal when she thinks, with a feeling of shame that slips down the backs of her legs like afterbirth, 'I wish to God I didn't send that invitation.' She's been in *People* with Madonna, *The Wall Street Journal* with Rabbi Berg, and *Architectural Digest* has photographed her home with her in it, but she has never thought that her family would want to find her. It's something else entirely to send an invitation. It was weak. It looked like she cared about them. Needed them in some self-serving, old-fashioned way.

Soon after coming to California, she had changed her name to something chic, easy to spell, free of barnyard odour – changed her name so nothing could reach out and catch her by her long black hair and drag her back to Wisconsin. There was something waiting to kill her in Avalanche.

Even after she ran away, she found herself staring out of windows, waiting, and once, during a double period of history back in high school, she had stared out at a snow-covered corn field for the entire two hours. Nothing moved. No bird flew over. No blackened stalks poked through the crust, no tracks crossed the field at an angle. Just as the bell rang, the north-westerly wind dusted a veil of snow down from the roof, and instead of heading for the lunchroom with her classmates, she pushed up the window and leaned out, feeling the fat in her cheeks harden as it froze. She waited, and as time passed, rolled her hands in the front of her T-shirt, exposing the bowl of her belly. The field remained empty, and she saw that the emptiness itself might be the thing that could kill her.

After school, a torn plastic grocery bag sailed unevenly over the field. It snagged on a dead elm, and fluttered there.

On her way home, Mike, the mailman, drove by without waving, and the next day she took the Greyhound bus in to Minneapolis.

When Mrs Appeldorn's husband steps out to talk dollars per pound with the driver of the bulk tanker, she dials 411. He would rather that she drive all the way to LaCrosse and browse the out-of-state phone books in the library than waste a dollar using directory information. He is a quiet man, and he has let her know his preferences in carefully penned messages on the margins of bills. He rarely shouts or loses his temper and has become even more placid and bovine with the passing years. When he's chewing his vegetables, she half expects a foamy green string of spit to dangle from the corner of his mouth. She stands next to the window, watching the two men move the discussion from money to off-colour jokes, and she is thinking how unsubtle her husband is, how his hand motions reveal every detail of the conversation, when the operator asks, 'What city and state, please?'

'San Francisco, California.'

'What name, please?'

'Gloria App. A, double p.'

'I'm sorry. There's nothing listed for that name in San Francisco.'

'Is there any listing for any other App? Not initial G?'

'There's one listing, Ma'am, but it's unpublished. Sorry.'

'Wait. Don't hang up. The one that's unpublished, is there an address for that one?'

'No. I'm sorry. Everything's unlisted.'

Small animal traps soak in the sink. Brown guard hairs and flecks of bone float on the surface of the rusty water, and a scaly black tail lies, dripping, in the dish rack. Mrs Appeldorn hauls a trap out by its chain and picks off tags of waterlogged flesh. On the stove, the muskrat she caught in the Kickapoo bobs in a soup of beer, mustard and onions. Steam from the open pot fogs the windows and the kitchen smells like Heileman's beer and wet skunk. She tries to forget Gloria saying, 'To err is human, to eat muskrat is not.'

'What do you think he looks like?' she asks, picking, picking, picking.

'Who?'

'Very funny. The wedding's in six days.'

'I wish you'd stop yapping about that stupid wedding.'

'Listen, Vernon, we have to go. She's our daughter.'

'Lee Wuornos was somebody's daughter too.'

'Gloria's not a serial killer.'

'That's bullshit. We haven't seen her in years. She hasn't cared enough to call in all that time. How do you know what she would and wouldn't do? You know nothing about her.'

'A mother knows her child.'

'Did you know she was going to run off?'

'God, I hate you sometimes.'

'When I win.'

'You didn't win.'

Mrs Appeldorn had waited for news from her daughter, until one day, in the seventh year, it occurred to her that Gloria was never going to write, didn't feel any kind of invisible umbilical cord connecting them, was – in all likelihood – an ex–Hare Krishna bag lady who didn't even remember her own name, and from that day, she had let the idea of Gloria float away. She thinks of her daughter now in the same way she thinks of her brother, who was killed sleeping in a seaplane lying at anchor in Broome in the far north-west of Australia, when Japanese Zeroes strafed the harbour. It was 9:30 in the morning, on Tuesday the third of

October 1942, and his body was not recovered with the others from the mangrove swamp where they were washed with the rising tide. She thinks of them both as stories, people who have strange things happen to them, people she doesn't really know.

But each October, she remembers her brother, standing in the warm el of her home, watching the combine weave its streamer of corn dust and smoke into the afternoon light, one crow calling to another, a maple leaf falling free from its burning building, red petiole dangling as it falls like the feet of a suicide, rotating and expanding as it blows towards her, platting against her cheek.

And in January, she remembers Gloria, hanging out washing on the line behind the house, the air still and wet and raw, the snow squeaky underfoot, the overalls in her hands smelling of gasoline.

Mrs Appeldorn is wiping spoons free of water spots before nesting them next to the others in the drawer. When her husband comes in from the barn, she says, 'I'd like to go in to LaCrosse today to get the tickets. If we wait any longer, we won't be able to get on a flight. Could you let me have the credit card?'

'Terrorists could hijack us and plough us into a field some place and Gloria wouldn't care.'

Her finger traces the ridges in the metal band that trims the red formica countertop. There are deep cuts in the formica, and a circular brown burn from the time when she took a pot from the stove without wearing an oven mitt and dropped it.

'Don't you want to meet your son-in-law?'

'No. He'll be some pansy, faggot, silk shirt fella, never saw a day's work in his life.'

'Give me the credit card, damn it!'

He runs his hand back through his hair and she sees his shirt is torn under the arm.

'The buckle on my overalls got bent in the washing machine. I used a rubber band to hold it yesterday, but it wants mending. Do you think you'll be able to get to it today?'

Before the wedding, Gloria has one final appointment with Rabbi Berg, spiritual head of the Kabbalah Centre, and leader of the fastest growing celebrity cult on the west coast. She is eager to discuss Chakra Healing, her phenomenally successful web-based business which sells crystals and also a new line in Zulu war paint, and her alien abduction. She meets him on a night when the moon is full, and he makes her stand, arms and legs spread, on a white sheet and gazes at the pale shadow she casts. One hand, her right, is missing from the shadow. No matter how she is repositioned, the hand is lost.

He asks, 'What is your mother's name?'

Gloria, startled, almost says 'Mommy', but then manages to squeak out, 'I'm not Jewish.'

'Mmm,' he says. 'What is she like, your mother?'

'Right before hunting season opens, my father paints an orange stripe down the back of anything that moves on his farm – cows, horses, the dog, Mom – just to be sure no one takes a pot shot at his precious livestock. He'd never leave to come to the wedding, and Mom won't come if he doesn't. She's his chihuahua. She'll wag her tail and pant over the invitation, but then she'll climb right back in Dad's pocket.'

'I take it you don't have a good relationship with them?'

An image stabs her: she is twelve, playing baseball with her parents after milking, the twilight sky a deep purple tent over their heads, the frogs in the pond just beginning their love songs. Her mother's wild pitch sails straight at her head, and her father's voice comes anxious from behind her, 'Steady, May. We want to keep this girl.'

And her mother muttering, 'Speak for yourself.'

'I haven't seen them in twenty years,' Gloria says to Rabbi Berg.

'Things can change.'

'I never want to be in anyone's pocket.'

'No risk of that.'

In the basement, Mrs Appeldorn unlocks the file cabinet and slides open the top drawer. Each folder is labelled in her husband's fussy handwriting, the g's looking like her father's wire -rimmed glasses, each i topped with a circle instead of a dot. The insurance policy is in a file towards the back. She pulls the entire folder out and inhales its odour of mildew and yeasty bread, a smell that makes her hungry and nauseous at the same time.

After Gloria disappeared, she began to stay up late, lining the claw-footed tub with her daughter's down quilt and lying cocooned in it, reading romances by kerosene lamp so as not to wake her husband, and sometimes a faint scent of Gloria would rise from the down, reactivated by body heat, or maybe just by her imagination, and on those nights, the bathmat knitted from plastic shopping bags and the towels turned and resewn down the middle seemed monstrous to her, and she had to fight the urge to tear them apart.

Now, she passes over the wills and the deed to their house, and, hoping that Gloria's fiancé is as financially responsible as Vernon, she slips out her husband's whole life policy. Stapled to the back page is a form for cashing out and claiming the accumulated value. Twenty thousand dollars.

From the phone in the laundry room, she calls the insurance company and is connected with a twittering female voice, which tells her that it takes up to six weeks to cash in a policy.

'Is there any way we can get the money faster? Our daughter's getting married in a week.'

'I just got married myself and the money flies out the door but I'll tell you what, honey. Fax the surrender form to me today, and I'll take care of it personally. We'll overnight the cheque to you and you'll have it in your hands before Friday. How's that?'

Against the basement window, she aligns the form over a cancelled cheque and traces her husband's signature. As she shapes the large A at the beginning of Appeldorn, she hears the tractor turn off in the machine shed, followed by the faint crunch of boots coming around to the kitchen door. She tries to hurry but her damp hand smears the letters and she has the sensation that her throat is swelling, closing, so that she can't get a single clean breath.

Vernon calls from the top of the stairs, 'May? You down there?'

'I'm trying to fix that buckle,' she says.

'I'm glad you're not upset about the credit card.'

'Oh, no,' she says, 'I was mad at first, but you're probably right.'

'That's my girl.'

'I don't think this buckle can be fixed. I'll head on over to Sparta this afternoon and see if they've got one.'

'Maybe you should bring it out to the shop before you go. I got that clutch working all right.'

The night after she faxes the surrender form, she is awakened by an odd noise in the wall and can't fall back asleep wondering what the sound reminds her of. Not mice, but perhaps keys turning in locks. Many keys in many locks.

Her husband's hearing aid, lit by the light from the clock, looks like a foetus she once saw in *National Geographic*, pink and glistening, folded in on itself. She considers driving to the all-night Walmart to look through their pattern books for something up-to-date, but as she mulls this over she suddenly knows that the sound she has been hearing is run-off trickling through the downspout on the other side of her bedroom wall, that this is the early spring rain that pocks the tired snow and causes the waiting earth to shiver and stretch, and she also knows she will buy a dress, because that would please Gloria.

She finds the dress at the Goodwill, a fifties chiffon in blues, an overlay of silvery lace with a neat self-belt and a round mother-of-pearl buckle at the pinched waist, most of the petticoats intact. It only needs the simplest of alterations to fit: taking in the seams at the bust and the waist, and relining the circle skirts with an old shower curtain. The dress is exactly right for a mother-of-the-bride, frilly, feminine, a bit glamorous.

Wearing the dress, she climbs the narrow, painted stairs to the attic. Light falls in bars on the floor, and as she shuffles to the hat boxes, particles of dust flash golden through the beams. She fossicks, opening box after box until she finds the hat she wore to Gloria's christening, a crescent-shaped metal frame covered in netting and blue silk petals, secured by tiny hand stitches. It is a little loose – she is shrinking inside her own skin – and she bends the wire gently between her hands, and this time it fits snugly over her coiled white hair.

Humming the Elizabethan Waltz, she spins like a mote, in and out of the light. The hat matches the new dress perfectly, the same dying blue as her eyes. Her son-in-law will love her in blue. Everyone loves her in blue.

'Gloria sent us tickets,' she lies. 'They came today.'

It's Friday night, two days before the wedding, and she is in bed beside her husband.

'What's that?'

He fumbles with his hearing aids, knocks one off the bedside table.

'I hate these stupid things.'

She feels like telling him it's his own fault. He should have worn headphones when he was out working with the noisy farm machinery. She feels like screaming that she has cashed in his whole life insurance, his only savings, so loudly that he'll hear it in his bones. She wants him to hit her, to put his fist through the wall and throw the old RCA radio through the window. An image of herself slicing plastic grocery bags into strips flickers before her in the darkness. Long, shrivelled ribbons of plastic squirm at her feet, clinging to her skirt, twisting in her hair, and one wriggling in the socket of her eye, rippling in the draft from the broken window. She hears singing, something slow in a minor key, without accompaniment.

'What did you say?'

She takes a breath.

'Gloria sent us tickets.'

'Like hell she did.'

'Really. FedEx dropped them off today.'

She can't believe he missed the truck in their driveway, idling as the driver handed over the certified cheque from

Northwestern Mutual. The exhaust had looked like an anaemic mushroom cloud.

'If you think that changes my mind, you've got another think coming. I'm still not going.'

'But she wouldn't send tickets unless she was really looking forward to seeing us.'

He is silent and, in the dark, she reaches for his hand.

'Right?'

'She can't do that to us. Like a stop light. Green. I love you. Red. I hate you. Green. I love you again.'

'Don't be so stubborn.'

'Gloria doesn't love you, May. The only person she's ever loved is herself.'

'You're just bitter.'

He pulls his hand away and rolls onto his side.

'No,' he says, 'I often wish that she died in a car accident so I could cry over her, think she called our names when she saw the headlights, but I know that isn't true. She was always cold. She used to cringe when you hugged her – her own mother, for God's sake. But you go if you want to.'

He sits up, and she hears his drawer shwuff open, papers whispering, and then a metallic clink and the snap of a rubber band. From behind he looks headless, just a set of broad shoulders in a patched nightshirt. The electric alarm clock daubs him with a bloody light, and there is a tiny click as the minute card inside its glass face flips down. Ten thirty-four.

'Here,' he says, turning, and he lays eight creased ten dollar bills in her hand. 'Get her a present.'

On the twin-prop plane from LaCrosse, a man drops into the seat next to her. He is wearing a suit and a red paisley bow tie, and as he pulls a laptop out of his briefcase, his perfumed sleeve brushes hers. She flicks through a bridal magazine bought with stolen money, looking at smiling faces and trying to subtly edge away. The roar of the plane's engines is no match for the roaring in her own head and she can barely hear him when he asks, 'San Francisco? International Film Festival?'

After she shakes her head, he asks, 'Gay and Lesbian Travel Expo?'

'What are you talking about?' she says. 'Do I look like one of those kind of people?'

She worries that this is what happens to people who travel alone. They become suspected deviants. All these years, she thought travelling with Vernon was a sign of their mutual respectability when, in reality, it only signalled her own lack of depravity.

The man's eyes drift from her trembling chin down to her shit-smeared orthopaedic shoes. 'No,' he says. 'No you don't.'

She turns the page and glares at a bride.

In San Francisco, she takes the shuttle from the airport to Union Square and walks to the Green Tortoise Hostel. From the window of her shared room, she sees neon lights advertising things she thought were illegal. Violent metallic crashings from a concert downstairs shake a rain of small insects off the ceiling and, alarmingly, they run for the bed and climb under the covers. After she dresses, she walks along Broadway and turns down toward the Embarcadero and Pier 33. The streets are full, roiling and boiling with people and cars, taut young men on bicycles darting between beeping trucks and rearing up unexpectedly on the sidewalk. It has been many years since she saw real black men and as she passes them, she sniffs their odour of foreign flowers and coconut, bright and hopeful against the squalid breeze from the Bay, a rotting mix of seal and salt and fish and diesel. She already wants to go home. Already knows from the air itself that Gloria will be unrecognisable.

The wedding is held on a yacht in the bay, the water unfathomably black and cold, the guests smoothly oiled and glittering. She's the only one tugging at her clothes, tripping over new shoes, waiting for a glimpse of her daughter. She hasn't found any other address for Gloria than the boat on this night. And the guests are all women. They wear backless tops with no sign of bra straps, and torn designer jeans, and expensive perfume that has never made it to Avalanche. The silver overlay on her dress looks nothing like the rhinestones swirling over their faded denim and if she could, she'd rip out her mildewed plastic petticoat and toss it overboard. She passes two women swaying in a stairwell, kissing. Not a social kiss. Vomit rises in her throat, together with other painful urges. Gasping, she sucks in the sweet smoke from the women's shared cigarette, a smoke that reminds her of the peculiar tangible stink of fermenting corn tassels.

'Excuse me,' she says, tapping the woman next to her, 'I'd like to meet the groom. Where is he?'

The woman lifts her wine glass to her eyes and stares at Mrs Appeldorn through it. She raises one eyebrow, and says, 'A vibrator?' Mrs Appeldorn backs away, trips over a rock. Stones have been arranged around the deck, lettered with fluorescent paint – the kind used on roadside reflectors, and, puzzled, she'd read them earlier: 'Survivor', 'Artist', 'Dreamer', 'Lover', 'Believer'. Bending over, she picks up a stone, cradling it, relishing its weight, its stony shoulders, its roundness in her hands. The word painted on it is 'Inspiring'.

She rubs the stone on her thigh, scratches spots never meant to be scratched in public, hawks and becomes the rube she least wishes to be. Gloria, spotting her from the bridge where she is adjusting her twenty-seven foot train studded with celestite – a crystal used in astral travel and in replacing pain with loving light – says, 'Oh God! What's she doing here?'

How utterly predictable that her mother should show up at the exact moment when she's least wanted, when Gloria is finally able to speak about Avalanche without feeling frostbitten, when – thanks to years of therapy – she has reached a place where she revels in her independence. And embarrassingly, her mother looks like a Romanian cleaning lady, an unfamiliar old refugee wearing rags and a dead man's smile like badges of survival. The boat is already well out in the bay, but if it weren't, she'd have someone ask her mother to leave. She'd even do it herself.

Unaware, Mrs Appeldorn creeps around the deck, overhearing fragments, partial sentences that are somehow focused and perfect like the momentary images frozen on the television screen when her husband clicks from channel to channel, searching for the loudest voices.

'It's not so strange. In Hindu countries, sick children are married off to dogs ...'

'Is Gloria's daughter here?'

'Dad's a postman back in Disaster or wherever.'

She is stunned that Gloria has a child. That she is a grandmother. She can't believe Gloria withheld even this from her, but she searches the crowd anyway, looking for a country girl with waist-length hair and black fingernails. She sees only California women, jeans wedged tightly in their privates.

When everyone is seated for the wedding, a bald woman

in a lime-green muu-muu and Doc Martens hefts the stones individually, reading each one aloud in a smooth radio voice, before dropping it over the railing, her fingers hanging like willow branches even after the splash. She stares at Mrs Appeldorn's rock, but doesn't ask for it.

The guests sit silently, serious and thoughtful. They appear to accept rock-throwing as a standard wedding practice, like cans behind the car, crudités, or confetti. Mrs Appeldorn twists around to look for the groom. She prays that there's a groom, any kind of a groom, and not a partner. Not a ... woman. She makes a little sound, a mew, or maybe it's more like a hiss. And she pokes her fingernail through the lace of her dress and rips at the shiny, silvery stuff while she waits. Shreds it.

The muu-muu woman leans down and fiddles with a boom box, which fills the air with an eerie recording of whale song. The guests ululate, the bride descends from the bridge and – oh! – she is lovely. The keening of the whales is accompanied by the stamping of young girls with cans of crystals tied to their ankles. Nobody notices the letters of God's holy and unknowable name that Gloria has inked on the train of her gown. Mrs Appeldorn waits for Gloria to turn, to notice her, to smile. The seals bark on Alcatraz.

Gloria walks around the canopy seven times, and then stands in front of the rabbi – a sleek Japanese woman in an elaborate kimono, the sleeves of which hang to her split-toed socks. Mrs Appeldorn stares at her with horror: how could Gloria forget that her own uncle, her mother's only brother, was killed by the Japanese? She feels like she is a sweater being incautiously unravelled from a dozen damaged places at once, the yarn piling at her feet in kinks and snarls. She feels nothing like the mother of the bride but stares hungrily at the bride anyway. Gloria's hair has been twisted into a unicorn's horn, wound with silver wire, polished emeralds, baby's breath, and dipped in green at the tip, as if she has deflowered a frog. The back of the gown is open to the base of her spine, where a tattoo of an upraised middle finger nestles in the valley between her buttocks. The train bumbles along behind her, gum wrappers and swizzle sticks tangled in the lacy edges.

A black-haired girl standing near Gloria whispers something to the rabbi and lifts a gilded mirror. Four candles gutter in the exhaust from the diesel engine, their light quivering oddly in the sequins of the bridal gown. Mrs Appeldorn strokes the rock as Gloria sips from the cup of wine, extends her index finger and the ring is slipped on. The ancient words, words that have joined two souls as one since time immemorial, but which are alarmingly unfamiliar to Mrs Appeldorn, are softly spoken – 'Behold! You are consecrated to me with this ring, according to the law of Moses and Israel.' – and the Japanese rabbi adds, 'Will you love this woman as your truly wedded wife in happiness and in sadness, in sickness and in health, honour her and cherish her until death do you part?'

The bay wind draws a cold finger down Mrs Appeldorn's spine as Gloria says, 'I do.'

'Then you may kiss the bride.'

Against her will, Mrs Appeldorn leans forward to get a better view, just as the women holding up the canopy lean forward with their candles, grease raining down on the hem of the gown like fat from side bacon, and she has a suddenly clear view of Gloria turning and tenderly kissing the mirror.

'What?' she thinks, not understanding.

Gloria stands alone in a ring of well-wishers, laughing. She pats the girl, takes the mirror from her and holds it up. The moaning of the whales is joined by the beating of drums, the panting of pan pipes, and the women gyrate, fused, grinding together, licking each other's faces, winking. The girls stamp faster and faster. The crystals crash in their cans. The boat rises rhythmically on the hips of the water. The air is suddenly hot. A woman with a buzz cut and barbed wire in one eyebrow undulates against Mrs Appeldorn, and whispers, 'Are you with someone tonight, or are you a do-it-yourself gal, like Gloria?'

Mrs Appeldorn's head sizzles and hums, wired and electric, tiny blue shocks snapping off the steel cage of her hat and exploding into rose petals that rain darkly on the tilting deck. With the lights on, her daughter looks like she is covered in broken glass. In each shard, she sees the shattered eyes of the night, thousands of shades of darkness, and she smoothes the stone, thinking of the day her husband taught her how to pitch. Her husband's hand over her hand over the softball. The eager, true flight of the ball and her husband's calm voice calling, 'Strike!' The stone moves, impatient, in her hand.

'Gloria!' she cries, as her arm swings back, her fingers groping for leather laces, her voice a seagull's scream.

The Resurrection of the Messiah

It had been seventeen uneasy days since the Messiah had arrived in the forgotten town of Wittenoom, a truck stop in the northwest of Australia, population twenty-seven. It had not been in the job description that he would have to make personal trips to places beyond the reach of modern communication devices. It had been quite sneaky, actually.

'But how hard could this be?' he gloated, as his donkey passed a sign announcing the presence of dangerous levels of airborne asbestos. 'Inhaling Will Cause Cancer,' the sign warned. He had forgotten or never known that the bones of many other Messiahs lay in this very ground.

The main street, indeed the *only* street, was graced with a pub: deserted, a roadhouse: boarded up with sheets of asbestos, and a knitting supply shop or something that looked like it tripled as the local betting agency and the lady's grog shop: likewise abandoned. Small asbestos cottages with rusting tin roofs stood between these, their wee yards frying pans of packed red dust.

When he grew tired of dodging the local mongrels, all of which seemed hell-bent on sniffing his crotch no matter how many times he pushed them away, he began calling out to the burghers, expressing himself as a gentleman and a Messiah should under such trying and generally disappointing circumstances. 'Hullo? Is anyone here? Is anyone at home? Don't be afraid. It is only I, your humble Saviour.'

He knew, as only a Messiah can know, that the entire population of twenty-seven were no longer in Wittenoom, had somehow ducked out on him and, in order for them to be saved, he would have to find them – his wayward sheep – and talk to them, convince them of his sincerity and his great and pressing desire for them to join his holy mission.

'Hullo?' he called again, without much hope, shoving away yet another one of the dogs, sweat trickling down inside his white robes, the donkey's hot body raising heat rash on his bare legs.

'Hullo?'

He cast his thoughts out, a radar peculiar to Messianic personalities, bounced them off the stacked Hamersley Ranges and deep into Wittenoom Gorge itself, sunk his God rays into every dessicated gully – of which there were many – in a twenty-mile radius, until he found all twenty-seven of the residents of Wittenoom clustered around a pit on a flat stretch several miles out of town. They appeared to be inebriated, all of them, and, as he mentally probed the scene, one of the citizens fell into the pit.

This sorry accident spurred him to a hasty decision, one he would later regret, especially upon his debriefing by The One Above, who had no great tolerance for flashy behaviour.

Billy Baggs saw the Messiah first, as a darker white spot against the deadly white of the noonday sun, and thought it might be time for that cataract surgery he had been pondering. Old Tony Mac was next, and all he saw were the donkey's legs floating miraculously down to earth, before he passed out facedown in the scorching dirt, causing himself to retain second degree burns to his hands and face, and no end of teasing. It was the booze that'd knocked him arse up in the dust, he'd say in later years, not the Unidentified Flying Donkey.

The others were slower to notice the apparition, as they were in the middle of burying one of their number, and they mostly had their eyes on the travelling priest, a man wearing short shorts, a black singlet and a pair of ancient elastic-sided Blunnies without socks.

'Righto, so we're here to bury our good mate, James Buggery ...'

'Jim!' said the dead man's wife.

'Butterworth!' shouted several of the dead man's friends.

'... an' he's been a bloody good mate, especially to his wife.'

This was in reference to Jim Butterworth's many children, and was greeted with stunned silence by all twenty-seven of the bereaved.

'A real trooper, I reckon, an' I wanna commend his soul to God.'

One of the mourners emptied a beer can into the grave and, at this, the priest took a sip from the bottle of plonk hung with the crucifix from his neck on a piece of twine, and he wiped his mouth on the hem of the singlet, exposing his pregnant and hairy belly in the process.

The Messiah shuddered as he saw a fleet of bush flies, pirates of the skies, attack the open neck of the bottle, stamp their tiny feet all over the rim, their feet that so recently had been stamping on the rotting bodies of sheep, the bloated bodies of goannas, the ordure of emus.

Bill Farr and 'Armless Hugh muttered together, still unaware of the Messiah standing directly behind them.

'Bloody mug of a priest. Jim was a whingeing bludger. Bloke's going straight to the hot spot.'

'Too right. He'll be toast, right about now.'

'But you'd think the bloody priest could at least get Old Jim's name right.'

Unwittingly, their voices had risen and the priest, annoyed, glanced in their direction and froze, his hand on the bottle. He continued to stare until, one by one, the inhabitants of Wittenoom, population twenty-seven, turned around to see what was so interesting to him that his mouth still hung open and a lone intrepid fly ventured in to stamp upon his tongue.

'Who the bloody hell are *you*?' said Jake Morris, speaking for all of them.

'Ah. Just the question I would expect from an inquiring mind. Who do I look like?' said the Messiah, head modestly bent in an attempt to channel the uncomfortable crown of thorns he'd finally pawned back in Shark Bay. A phosphorescent glow rose from his swaying donkey.

'A towel-head, I reckon!'

'Lawrence of bloody Arabia!'

'A flamin' fruitcake!'

'Look out, mistah! Your donkey's about to cark it!'

And with that, the donkey that had carried him so faithfully and so far, keeled over, and the Messiah leaped nimbly free and landed catlike on his soft, unshod feet.

And screamed! And cried! And danced! And finally threw the white cloth from his head onto the ground and stood on it, blisters rising on his tender feet. It could now be seen that he had a head of long, curly red hair, and the men began to point at him and snicker. Between the trailing white dress and the girly hair, the men of Wittenoom had decided that here was one of those faggots come from who-knows-where for the express purpose of their entertainment.

It was an inauspicious start.

The Messiah, however, was a veteran of many inauspicious starts, not the least of which was that nasty business in Jerusalem, and his image had always been resurrected. He was nothing if not confident.

'Now gentlemen, though this may come as somewhat of a surprise to ones so poorly educated in the spiritual arts as yourselves, I am here as your annointed one, your Messiah ...'

'Yeah, you an' every other nutjob down from Roeburne.'

'Yer donkey's carked it, mate.'

'I'll skin it for ya, only cost ya a bob.'

And the voice of the priest over all, 'I've et a fly!'

The Messiah could feel the heat in the ground rising like lava from a volcano through the head-cloth and pouring over his mortified feet, and from above, the sun bored into his fair skin, an unfair challenge if ever there was one, scorching the fine hairs on his arms to ash, a billion BTUs intent on cooking him *all the way through*. In every direction, as far as he could see, there was no shade, just miles and miles of the stunted blue-grey spinifex, knee-high and dusty. He thought of raising a tree, an English oak here in the Australian desert, or maybe producing a fountain of cool water, or even a simple little rain cloud, but he knew from past experience that his best chance for success with the locals would be to raise the dead man, and this he did with a glance.

It was only as the dead man climbed out of the pit, raining maggots and shreds of putrid musculature, a blizzard of flies cloaking his privates and an unforgettable odour emanating from the fluids that leaked from his many orifices, that the Messiah got a clear picture of the full extent of his mistake.

'Shit!' he said, and he kicked the donkey.

The Decline and Fall of Drusilla Ann Gherkin

In the summer of 1972, Drusilla Ann Gherkin, twelve years old and ninety-eight kilograms, waited for her voice to break. She waited in her hot and itchy polyester shift, a maternity dress her mother hemmed up to fit her squat frame, her neck ballooning over the lace collar. Her sisters told her that her voice would break, change from its hoarse and manly baritone to a more feminine note, on the day she turned thirteen. She had been waiting for February 2, 1973, since she was eight. It sucked, how slowly time moved.

Her sisters, Kitty and Kar, tall and slim, already beautiful in that dying way of teen girls, shunned her company, her redolent body odour, her bewarted hands, and called her Dag, an acronym of her initials that was also the word for a hanger-on, derived originally from the foul, matted clumps of excrement that dangle from a sheep's rear end.

'Get away from me, Dag. You give me the heaves.'

'Your guinea pigs are running away, Dagwood!'

She would dash off to check on her piglets even though she was sure her sisters were lying, because she loved those humble little beasts that loved her back, warts and all. And at night, she dreamed of becoming a guinea pig, a huge guinea pig that could fly, a rodent superhero.

On this day, February 1, the day before her thirteenth birthday, she dressed in her pale blue Speedo swimsuit with the modesty flap. The previous evening, she had inked a large black S on the chest. It looked fabulous. She pinned a bath towel to her shoulder straps to complete the ensemble and presented herself for breakfast.

'My God, darling,' said her mother, 'you have *four* buttocks!'

'What's that you're wearing, Dagwood?' asked Kar, eating peanut butter from the jar with a spoon.

Super Guinea pulled the towel around to cover the bulge of her bust and the lurid S.

Kitty twitched the towel away and snorted.

'Super Fatso, is it?'

'Super Fartso!'

Drusilla Ann tried to snatch the towel back. Her sisters, both lithe and both fuelled on high-octane torment-juice that they kept chilled in a big pitcher in the fridge, danced just out of her reach. Oh, the futility of it all. As she lumbered from Kitty to Kar and back again, her arms came free and began to windmill and snatch at the girls, but this, regrettably, revealed what she had wished to hide.

Her family ogled the S.

She crossed her arms over her chest.

'I'm Sooooop-er Guinea!' Her voice cracked on 'Guinea'. Beads of sweat trembled on the fleshy inner fold of her red ears. She kept her eyes trained on the edge of the counter.

Kitty and Kar cavorted around the kitchen flapping their sarongs, shouting 'Sooooop-er Guinea!' Each time they spotted Drusilla Ann in her superhero swimsuit, they howled with laughter. Their beaks snackled and snapped at her. Mrs Gherkin, muffling her own snorts, walked behind Super Guinea and twitched her daughter's wicked wedgie out from between the cheeks of her buttocks.

'Mummy!' wailed Drusilla Ann. She clamped her moist hands over her butt, leaving sweat prints.

'Dag's just cranky 'coz Mum's found out why she's so fat... she's got *two* mouths ... one above and one below.'

'That's yucky, Kar. I don't want to hear that kind of talk,' said their mother, but she was laughing when she said it, so it didn't count.

Kitty held up two fingers and pointed them at Drusilla Ann. She could wiggle her ears but tried not to nowadays, as Kar had told her that it caused those wrinkles old women get around their mouths, where the lipstick runs into the gorges and their mouths end up looking like squashed spiders made of unravelling chenille. Kar's beak flared as if she had skunk-flavoured gum stuck right under the nostrils. Drusilla Ann nibbled at a cauliflower wart on her knuckle.

Her sisters lacked a certain dignity and neither of them had any imagination.

After a minute of bending low into the fridge, her back shaking, her mother rose and handed her a bowl of Special K, dotted with banana, topped with an onion dome of heavy cream, and Drusilla Ann sanctified it with a ladle of sugar. When her mother left to do laundry, Super Guinea popped a wee dram of wart into her mouth, and then had seconds of the cereal and thirds of the cream. Cream, she had heard, was a balm to the vocal chords.

After breakfast, she worked at perfecting her champion's leap, running up to the pool, shouting 'Sooooop-er Guinea!' and cannonballing into the glittering water. Although the girls at school said that can openers made a bigger splash, that was only true if, indeed, your body resembled a can-opener, but not if your basic anatomy was cannonball. Her guinea pigs lolled in their cages alongside the pool, watching their hero, their red eyes unblinking.

When they'd eaten lunch, her sisters came to watch her bombs.

'She's faster than a bitch on heat!'

'More powerful than an egg burp!'

'Able to leap tall obstacles on the way to the fridge!'

'Sooooop-er Guinea!'

Years before, Drusilla Ann had perfected deafness. She saw their lips moving, but hadn't learned to lip-read.

'Zhlushwaaawaaaa!'

'Miggywimpysloompyslurp!'

'Larruppuppy!'

'Glomp!'

She feigned muteness when strangers visited the house, and, if forced to speak, covered her mouth with her fist so it might appear that the monstera deliciosa in the corner was a ventriloquist. The monstera was obviously part of the Mafia, what with its fleshy leaves and playboy bunny flowers and the hideous pinky ring doodad which tied it to a stake, and everyone knew that Mafia-types spoke with the kind of hoarse voice that emerged, horrifyingly, from behind Drusilla's hand.

There had been a girl in her school for a year, a girl from England, with black hair and white skin and eyes the exact colour of the sky a half-hour before dark in the summer. Alison was quiet and played the cello and had a kite from Indonesia hung from the ceiling of her bedroom. She'd invited Drusilla Ann home to see *her* guinea pig, an unusual bald variety, and Drusilla Ann had prepped herself, showering, using her mother's deodorant, twice, and dressing in the least bestial of her frocks. Alison gave her a slice of seed cake and asked several times what she was thinking about, as if she really cared. Drusilla Ann told her that she was thinking about her, Alison, about how pretty she was, and Alison put out her hand and rested it on Drusilla Ann's broad and warty palm without flinching, and said, very softly, 'You look so strong,' and for once, Drusilla Ann hadn't raised her fist to cover her mouth when she replied, 'I could carry your cello to school for you.' And all that year, she had.

That summer of 1972, the summer after Alison returned to England, Drusilla Ann didn't speak to anyone human. She made plays for her guinea pigs and promoted her favourite, Liddle Porker, to be her sidekick, Robin to her Batman, Tonto to her Lone Ranger, Porker to her Super-Guinea. The little pig scratched at the handkerchief tied cape-like at his neck. He shivered as he was flown across the pool and winced when her booming baritone was sounded too close to his tiny ears. He was pronounced upon by the sisters, to the theme music from Batman: 'Da-da da-da da-da da-da, Fart-man!' Truly, no imagination whatsoever. They would become uneducated women who spent two hours on Tuesdays getting manicured by Tibetan girls with PhDs, and they would still feel superior, despite the drug-resistant fungus that would set up shop on their nail beds and fornicate all over their cuticles. They would tell their own children not to say *fart*, but they would still think the word was funny. They would be ashamed to appear before company in honest glasses and would poke sharp pieces of clear plastic into their eyes every morning for the next sixty years rather than let anyone know they were flawed human beings. Idiots.

February 2, 1973, her birthday of birthdays, dawned quiet and hot. Drusilla Ann cautiously opened her eyes and gulped in a great lungful of the baked air. She could feel it eddying around her vocal chords, caressing her throat with warm and gentle hands, *healing* hands, God damn it. She cleared her throat and it seemed she could hear a difference. It seemed easier to swallow. In the bathroom, she looked at herself in the mirror and adjusted the towel on her shoulders. It was a new red towel. She turned from side to side to admire the effect. Snappy. She smiled and bowed low, once, twice, both times waving her hand to her audience, the tiles. They cheered and she smiled again. Her teeth were unusually small and pale grey as a result of some drug her mother had been given when Drusilla Ann was still swimming inside her stomach. Gross thought. The swimming, not the teeth. Her teeth were kind of interesting rather than nasty. She'd always thought that if she couldn't be pretty, at least she could be interesting.

She dodged questions at breakfast in order to preserve her feminised birthday voice for her entourage, shook her head when asked if she'd like to get her presents, and then hustled outside to line up her guinea pigs at the edge of the pool. She was thirteen at last and finally going to morph into the kind of person the beautiful girls at school might notice. The kind of person her mother might love. The ends of the red towel rose into the air and flapped, whispering *run run run*. There wasn't a particle of wind, she was sure.

She stood on her tiptoes and then, clad in her pale blue swimsuit with the S and the modesty flap, towel fluttering like wings behind her, her thick arms pumping, her thighs slapping, her breath all the way up in her forehead, she ran across the concrete deck, yelled out 'Sooooop-er Guinea!' in a voice unchanged by birthdays, and fell flat on her face in the deepest water of the pool.

Her sisters saw the towel later, on the washing line, dripping red dye, and told their mother that Drusilla Ann had ruined it.

Raw Milk

They walked down the hill each morning, mother and daughter trailing streamers of fog, the renaissance light of dawn tangled in the spider webs swinging between the goldenrod.

'Do you think they're up?'

'They're up.'

Two girls sat on their heels in the entrance to the barn, the hems of their dresses twitched away from the gutter, dark scarves knotted under their chins, one face freckled, one not. They picked shit and prickers from between their bare toes.

Without speaking, the girls took their places on either side of the cow, the freckled one tying the cow's saturated tail to the overhead beam, the other wiping the cow's teats. They butted their fists gently into the cow's udder, we're calves, they said, feed us, and her milk rang in the singing bucket.

A man, the father of these two girls and six other children, stepped out of a stall and scraped his boots on the lip of the gutter. Twin wedges of manure, undigested flakes of hay projecting from the surface, fell into a pool of horse piss and paper towels used to wipe the cow's teats. He turned to his neighbours, English folk come to buy his milk, a mother and daughter, their feet arranged awkwardly around liquid pats of cow dung.

'Hey, Polly. Winnie.'

One corner of his mouth turned up like it was caught on a

fish hook and his teeth shone in the dim light like scales.

'Good morning, Roman. How's Alvin these days?' Alvin was his only son, a boy who had been sick for over a year with cancer.

'Can't complain, but we're thinking it might be from them computer chips the guvmint says you gotta put inside of every animal. How do they know it won't be causing all kinds of problems?'

As he spoke, he drew spider webs from the black oak beams, and rolled them between his palms. He put the webs to bed in his pocket, muttering, 'Good for bleedin', and he would know, having picked his four right-hand fingers out of the sawdust one promising fall day last year.

And the mother and her child were used to the Amish man asking them what the world thought, as if they were God, or at least the god of the city, and privy to the thoughts of strange men in black suits and ties who owned bathtubs and electric toothbrushes.

'That's ridiculous! It sounds like they want to perch in your outhouse and spy on everything you do.'

'Ya, we reckon it might kill the critters, the chip. We seen some pretty weird things lately, calves with two heads and such.' Boys with leukaemia.

One of the girls milking the cow looked up, snapped her fingers. 'Lassie!' she hissed, surprise and disappointment in her voice, and their matted collie, scrounger of affection, slunk out from under the woman's hand.

'That one takes advantage,' said the Amish man. His girls smiled, but then ducked their heads into the cow's flanks when they noticed the two strangers did not think it was funny.

The freckled girl, Mary, carried the bucket to the basement

of the farmhouse, where the previous day's milking cooled in a stone sink full of water, and the mother and daughter followed her.

'Tastes better right after you change the water,' said Mary, squatting to strain the milk. 'Smells awful like mice down here, don't it? Mam's gonna bring the tabby soon, but mice or cats, both of 'em likes to drink milk.'

To the mother and daughter, the basement wallowed in the smell of sour milk, luxuriated in it, daubed it in every secret pulse point, every dark corner, and there was also the faint odour, the peculiar metallic whiff of the cast-iron chip heater used to burn dairy filters and bloody rags. Assaulted as they were, their olfactory senses were incapable of distinguishing the odour of mice.

'I reckon you know and I wouldn't have to tell you, but the milk tastes funny if you put the lid on before it cools.' Mary left the lid cocked on the can and jerked her head towards it. 'That'll be a dollar.'

They walked back to their cottage, the daughter carrying the lid, the red plastic bail of the full two-gallon can cutting deeply into the mother's palm, and they could hear the telephone ringing as they came up the hill. The girl ran ahead to answer it.

'I understand you have raw milk available? It's marvellous for the digestion, the perfect gut food, full of biotic life. But I'm sure you know that. Don't you? Well,' said the glittery voice, Chicago, Milwaukee, Minneapolis, 'I'd like to book a cottage for a week. A holistic spa for the flora in my colon. But I need to know one thing.'

'Yes?'

'Are the rooms clean?'

The girl paused. 'Oh, yes. Everything is all clean when you come.'

'That'll be fine then. You'd never believe it, but last summer – it was horrible – we rented a place in the country, and it had spiders.'

The girl lifted a web from the window sash and rolled it gently under one finger.

'Oh yes,' she said, 'I could believe it.'

C.H.A.R.M.I.N.G.

Dedicated to the memory of the real Harriet.
Truth is stranger than fiction.

June 4th

My doctor gave me the good news today. He said, 'Harriet, you've done it again. Despite your best efforts to smoke yourself to death, the scans are all clear,' and he laughed his desiccated little doctor's laugh, all malpractice and no mirth.

So, cancer has failed twice to kill me off. I am delighted. My sisters need me.

And I see this news as a gift from my mother, coming as it does on the anniversary of her death: I get to play house some more.

June 5th

I've been wondering why I've been spared. Seventy-six is an adequate amount of time on this earth, and I've read so many names in the obits, people who are younger than me, younger by far, and it leads me to believe that God has some plan for me. I have heard that we are here for seventy, eighty years, just to do a favour for another person, and surely I have done that, surely I have some merit in protecting my sisters, in trying to raise them. And yet my life has been so ordinary, nothing following nothing following nothing until it seems unbearably self-indulgent to think there has been a purpose to all these meaningless days.

O'Hare, Blossom

Blossom O'Hare, aged 80, was a remarkable patron of the arts, a tireless supporter of good causes and a perennial presence at cultural gatherings. She was as loyal as she was obstreperous, as cheerful as she was hardworking.

Blossom O'Hare passed last week at a nice even eighty. I read about her yesterday in the waiting room. Everyone wrote how nice she was, but to tell you the truth, she was a crazy old bat, the kind of woman who might have had senile dementia since she was a teenager. I'm glad she's dead.

June 6th

I notice that when I write, details flood my mind and my memory grows clearer. Does that happen to everyone?

Or am I just inventing it as I go along?

I pray that no one gets hold of this notebook after I'm dead. My nieces would love to get their claws on our family history. Names and dates, bits of lace, grainy photographs, all the people in funny clothes. Ha! They have no idea. The real story is in my bones.

June 7th

The stupid, obese, slow-moving and infinitely infuriating black nurse parked my chair in front of the window this morning and forgot about me. I wanted to wheel to the nurses' lounge and kick her with my deadly orthopaedic shoe. I called and called but ever since the throat cancer my voice has been nothing but a croak. No one came. My face and hands are sunburned and hurt like hell. I'm not going to write any more today.

Where are my cigarettes?

June 8th

Did I really say I think God has a plan for me? And does it have anything to do with *cooking* me?

June 9th

Maguire, Frederick

Fred Maguire, aged 78, of Hamden, CT, died June 9. The first American to climb the Sur-no-Gama, an active volcano in Persian Baluchistan, and a competent Poker player. Faithful husband and loving father. Survived by his only son, Digby.

I woke up today to the sounds of the aide trying to flush the goddam toilet, the ceramic scrape as she hauled off the lid to find out what was wrong and the sound of her discovering my cigarettes in their Ziploc baggie, floating in the tank like Moses in the basket. Damn.

Now, Moses' mother was someone I can respect ... despite the decree of the knee-high Pharaoh – 'Kill all the boys!' – she still dreamed up salvation for her child, floated him to safety in the arms of the black Egyptian princess; a princess, I might add, who did *not* proclaim, 'Caught you again, you wicked old thing!' when she drew the basket from the yellow waters of the Nile.

My mother died when I was twelve, incapable of dreaming up any kind of salvation for her children, floating in her own yellow river. My father had already been dead for three years. No loss. He was a loud alcoholic, the kind of man who'd chase his daughters with his pants down not meaning anything by it. My mother was retarded and never spoke, or only once that I know of.

I have to go over Ida's bank account. I think the aide is writing cheques to herself, believing that Ida has been abandoned, instead of being the beloved youngest of five sisters. Fool! She must be related to my own dark beauty of a nurse, a graduate of the Golem School of Chiropody, no doubt.

There was an obit for Fred Maguire in the Sunday papers. I put it in my scrapbook for a laugh. Whoever they paid to write 'Faithful husband and loving father' has obviously never noticed the large number of Fred Maguire look-alikes around town. They left out the condolences from his best friend, Jack Daniels, too.

June 10th

Ida's aide *was* writing cheques to herself. Bye bye, black bird.

I've been fretting over Ida's woes all day, even though I know she was marked for misery from the first, landing on her head that way.

When Mother died, Ida was only three. We had known for a while that our baby girl was slow. She drooled. I'd tie Dad's big hankies around her neck to sop up all her spit. We didn't know she had the Huntington's then. Of course we didn't. Showed up when she was thirty-four. I have to admit she was a sweet baby. The day she was born, I sent Rosa for the midwife but the old hag wouldn't come because she hadn't been paid for the previous birth.

Mother was quiet, never spoke really, and I only knew she

was having a hard time birthing Ida from the way she rolled her head from side to side. She had bitten her lip through without making a sound, there was blood on her face and what with the sweat and the stink and her eyes showing white, it was hard to look at her.

She surprised me by jumping off the bed and crouching on the floor, eyes glittering like that dreadful monkey they have over at the zoo. So evil, a bad spirit, little hands busy killing fleas. Ida fell out in a fine spray of blood, hitting the floor headfirst, and a minute later the placenta came out too. I thought it was another baby at the time, but I know better now. I was with Rosa and Marsha when they had their babies and I heard the doctors say 'Here comes the placenta.' Each time I stood there holding the raw baby with tears running down my face, remembering that time, always that time with Mother, and wishing with my whole heart that I didn't.

Mother looked down; touched that wet scrap of baby on the head, and got back into bed. She left the baby on the bedroom floor. I'll never forget that.

June 11th

That black nurse better not read my notebook or I'll kill her. The last thing I need is half this Home laughing at me. If you are reading this, Krystal, I will use the bread knife on you, and for your information, my cigarettes are inside the smoke detector. Ha!

June 12th

I wrapped Mother's baby up in a towel, together with that big mess of afterbirth – I've never been able to eat tomato soup since – and I put her in a drawer. I was seven years old and knew things needed to be named, so I asked Mother what to call the baby. She just stared at me with those glittery black animal eyes.

Ida's aide has been dismissed. How stupid can you get, writing cheques to yourself?

June 13th

Mildred Glimperdink's shitzu assistance dog
nose-punched a telephone's 911 button upon
seeing Glimperdink suffer a massive colon prolapse
and then he barked furiously into the phone.

Tattletale.

It looks like Krystal isn't reading my diary, or if she is, she doesn't want me to know, because my cigarettes are still safe in their hiding place.

Since discovering that the cancer didn't get me, post-polio has decided to take a shot. I feel like someone switched my legs for two broomsticks in the night.

June 14th

Last night, I tried to kick one of my legs out of bed, thinking it was a dog or a baby or something unwanted, thinking I needed to send it *elsewhere*, and I woke up thick with the memory of how I made the others all wait in the cemetery while Ida was getting born. It was just over the road from us, a big grassy place, a perfectly good place to play. Marsha must have been walking around over there, chasing Rosa and Anita, glad she had a pair of new brown shoes. Chuck got those for her. They were sticking out of a box in someone's garbage. He'd had this idea of how to get clothes and shoes and things. In the paper, he saw those sad, sad poems parents write about their newly dead children. He wrote down their names, looked up their addresses in the telephone directory and then ran over there after work to pick through the trash. Some people mind about using a dead person's things, especially a dead child, and some people have qualms about taking things out of a garbage can. Not us. Marsha's shoes were almost new, they even had all the buttons.

June 15th

Well, the funniest things do come out when I write in this notebook. I'd forgotten about those shoes but that's probably how I got hooked on the obituaries. Never missed a day in at least fifty years. That and the crossword.

We didn't put an obit in for Dad. Too expensive by half and what could we say? That the man could barely keep his pants up?

He had named us all so our first initials spelled out CHARM; Chuck, Harriet, Anita, Rosa, Marsha; we had had CHARM until Ida was born, and even then we were on the way to CHARMING, but without Dad there wouldn't be an N baby, a G baby.

Just like him to suddenly croak, right when there was a new baby on the way. If there's one thing I remember about him, it's that he was always a bit surprised and disappointed with the results of his noisy canoodling. Right before Ida, he'd said enough was enough. He spoke to a vet he knew in the meat business, and asked if there was some operation they could do on Mother. Like castrating a bull calf, only different.

He was a big man with big grasping hands. Made a big crash when he hit the floor. His boots had shiny nails in the bottom of them, winked like eyes, and if he kicked you with them, you stayed kicked. I remember the boots and the feel of them on my backside better than I remember his face.

Mother didn't care to get up to see what'd made that noise, but Chuck and I came running and there was Dad, face down on the floor. He'd peed himself and it smelled like he'd done the other too and we started laughing because it looked like he was drunk again, or maybe we were just laughing because we were children. We were children then.

I must have a thousand, easy a thousand, obits here in my scrapbook and I can tell you that not a one says the deceased died swimming in their own pee, lathered in shit, but they all do. They all do.

Chuck got a bucket of water and threw it over Dad. I tried to prop up Dad's head and jam a pillow under it, and that's when I got a good look at his face and knew for sure he wasn't drunk, knew he wasn't going to be making an N baby or a G baby.

Our next-door-neighbour, a man who had the twitchies from Huntington's – the only other person I've ever known with that rare, directly inherited disease besides my own two sisters, however that is a point on which I'd rather not dwell – came over and made the arrangements for Dad's burial. None of us went to the funeral, but we climbed up on the roof and watched. The cemetery was conveniently right across the road from our house. Did I write that already?

Mother didn't go either. She was too far-gone pregnant, and besides, I don't think she ever left the house. I'm not sure if she knew that Dad had died. To be honest, I'm not really sure that she ever knew who Dad was.

My nieces would love to get their claws on this story, but

I've held it close for sixty years and they're not going to get it. They'd drag my poor old mother round in front of people who'd laugh at her. Nowadays you don't hear about retarded girls getting married and having six kids without knowing how it all happened.

June 16th

Dad was how it all happened, of course.

Anita's coming over this afternoon and I've got Diet Coke and some good diabetic cookies from the bakery on Whalley Avenue for her to eat. I'm going to ask her if she remembers what colour Dad's eyes were. I don't.

June 17th

She doesn't remember either.

Anita is getting hard of hearing though. She kept talking, right over the top of whatever I was saying and that's not like her. It was mostly glop about her girlfriends at the group home, and their nieces and nephews, and occasionally, 'Put out that butt, Harriet. You mightn't care about dying of lung cancer, but I do.'

She doesn't need to worry about lung cancer getting her. I already know how she's going to go. She'll be standing in the kitchen, before the aides are up, frying an egg, something she learned to do in the retarded class, and she'll wonder why she's sweating, why her arm hurts so bad, and they'll find her there, legs splayed, egg congealing on the floor, a melted place on the linoleum where the pan landed. She's got heart attack written all over her.

Anita will never notice that her hearing is all cockeyed. I'll have to make an appointment for her over at Yale New Haven and, even after the tests, she'll be surprised when they tell her she needs hearing aids.

June 18th
Rosa called to see how I am. What does she think? A telephone call from California is all it takes to be part of a family? I told her I think God spared me for a purpose and she *snorted.* I distinctly heard her snort. All that California psychobabble nonsense has made a mush of her brain. Maybe she thinks the little plastic Buddha she keeps on her shelf runs the world, but honey, that thing says 'Made in Taiwan' right on the bottom. It's God's perfect revenge that she has all those Hassidic grandchildren.

Baumwohl, Samuel

Sam Baumwohl, aged 74, was a sailboat enthusiast,and much-loved figure among the children of New Haven, where he founded the Pirate Club and was fondly dubbed 'Long John Silver' by its members.

They'll be saying kaddish for Sam right around now. *Yisgadal veyiskadash shmei rabbah.* Great and holy is His name. God's, that is, not Sam's; his was mud around these parts. Sam put his finger on the scale if you weren't looking and even if you were, and he dared to call himself a religious man. Religiously stole from his customers. A real mitzvah to steal from orphans but then, I'm forgetting that he didn't know we were alone.

June 19th
When we were younger we spoke the *mame loshen*, the mother tongue. All except Mother of course. The public school we went

to overflowed with the exuberant Yiddish-speaking offspring of Russian immigrants. Jabber jabber jabber. From the five Weiner sisters, I am the only one who remembers any Yiddish. I overheard Anita ask for *chein* the other day, unaware that instead of asking for horseradish, *chrein*, she had asked for charm.

Slurp. Just like that, poured into the melting pot and poured out as identical, sanitised, foil-wrapped Americans. Our family got all the dinged-up ones, the ones that were rejected because of damages. Still sweet on the inside, is what I say.

June 20th

Nary has a day gone by when I don't have to check up on Anita, Marsh, Ida. Even Rosa. She's coming apart at the seams and doesn't even know her stuffing's showing. Says she has to have her own space, but when she calls, no matter what she's saying, it's all crying, 'Lonely! Lonely!'

Yesterday, old-what's-his-name-the-second-husband took Marsha for a check-up and it turns out her Huntington's is getting worse. What a surprise. Upped her meds, so now, instead of looking like a stunned mullet nailed to a wheelchair, she'll be looking like a stiff stunned mullet nailed to a wheelchair toting an oxygen tank. I curse this rotten disease for all that it's done to my poor sisters. Marsha used to get men's attention; she was our voice, our emissary to the world of love. Now her own daughters avoid visiting her, can hardly look at her. They put their babies in her lap and as soon as those new souls feel her skin like a death, they howl, 'Lemme out of here! Something's bad wrong!' Her girls sit there, soaked in sweat, too afraid to get the test that will tell them if this will be their fate too, if their own children will hate them for this terrible inheritance.

What a life she's had. Married a man who ran off with another man. I suspected right from the start – he was an interior decorator, and they all seem to have that proclivity. Huntington's right after that and we thought she was just shook up, nervous and unhappy, her arms and head jerky with distress instead of chromosomes. And of course, our wonderful childhood, which in some ways truly was, but mostly wasn't. She must have been diabolical in a past life to deserve this one. We all must have been.

I'm going to install a ramp to make it easier for old-what's-his-name to wheel her in and out of the house. It's only one step up, but I'd hate for him to trip and let her fall.

June 21st

My sister-in-law, Lillian, died this morning.

June 22nd

Chuck always loved Lillian. I never knew what he saw in her. She complained that she married into a family of jealous girls who idolised their brother. Well, it's true. Chuck was everything to me, to us.

When Mother died, Chuck was fourteen, had already been working full-time for three years, peeling potatoes in Bernie's Restaurant. Got up at five o'clock for his paper route, dragged himself back at night after washing up at the restaurant. Gave every penny he earned to us until he was twenty-four and married Lillian, and even then, even then, fed us girls in his restaurant until he retired.

He was a beautiful man.

Not physically of course. None of us have that particular gift. Tall, thin, breath from the crypt, bad dandruff, false teeth, psoriasis, a lifetime of deli sandwiches rounding his shoulders.

But I felt when I was near him that I was protected. Loved even. Oh, I know that's an exaggeration. I'm not exactly lovable. But that's the kind of man he was.

Like I said, a beautiful man.

He died two years ago.

Lillian collapsed after that; didn't even call up to fight with me. All the spunk went out of her. She was just an old lady with badly dyed red hair.

Anita went to visit her every couple of days but poor Lillian couldn't stand hearing the same conversation over and over, being asked constantly how her bowels were, and I had to tell Anita to stop, that Lillian was fine, even though a greater lie was never told between me and my sister.

I'm going to have a cigarette while I'm lying here in bed.

I'm so tired tonight.

June 23rd

Chuck told Lillian about Mother being dead right before their wedding. That was the first time we'd told anyone. I expect Lillian was pleased not to have a mother-in-law looking over her shoulder. Just us girls.

After we buried Mother, we knew we didn't want to move, really badly didn't want to move away from our house, so I left school too and started working and we used the extra money to pay off the house and keep Rosa in school.

I got a job a few days after my twelfth birthday. When my teacher came round to our house, wanting to complain to Mother, of course we couldn't let her. I kept her standing on the porch and told her mother was feeling poorly, an understatement if ever there was one. She held my hand and said, 'Harriet, you're the best student I've ever had at Hillhouse ... can't your family find some way to keep you in school?' and I can tell you that was a painful thing to hear. Who wants to hear something like that when they're working in a deli, cutting roast beef, pastrami, corned beef, pickles? Some nights I'd go to bed smelling of good honest meat with nothing but oatmeal in my belly and a cold wind blowing down my back, a sure-fire recipe for sleeplessness.

Orenstein, Odelle Millicent

Odelle Orenstein, aged 92, died June 22 at the Jewish Home for the Aged. She leaves no survivors.

I've got the obit from Odelle Orenstein, the owner of that first deli, and I notice there are just the bare facts of her life writ there. No personal messages from family and friends. It reminds me of one of the headstones in the cemetery, leaning sideways from a hundred years of frost heave, the inscription mossed over but readable:

Poorly lived,
And poorly died,
Poorly buried,
And no one cried.

Not that the dead sit around in Hell, reading their own obituaries, and checking out the attendance at their funerals, but it's a sad thing and I hope someone will still be around to write some distortions about my life after I'm gone, along the lines of 'Harriet Weiner, extraordinarily devoted sister, survivor of just about everything, chain-smoker. She was needed.'

June 24th

I had that bad dream again. I told Rosa about it and she changed the subject. She's a psychologist. You'd think she'd know what it means.

In it, I am twelve again. My legs are round and healthy, carry me easily, my arms swing smoothly by my sides. I am revelling in this long-forgotten muscle dream as I walk around our house to the garbage cans. A cloud of flies rises up from one without a lid. In glorious slow-motion, I stoop to retrieve the cover and begin to replace it. I look down. There is a baby in the garbage. It is a newborn baby, naked, black with flies and tea leaves and ash.

Why am I dreaming this dream? What does it mean? I am too old to have babies. My aide asked me in her inconsiderate way if I ever wanted children and I told her, 'I did have children, five of them, and I raised them too.'

She is so obtuse. I am not sure if she realised I meant my sisters and my brother.

June 25th

Today is Lillian's funeral. Rosa can't come. She's morbidly busy in California it seems. I had the cemetery people lay out wooden boards next to the grave for all the wheelchairs. It's been raining and I have no plans on staying permanently at the cemetery. Yet.

I've got my cigarettes in the pocket of my good black coat. Sometimes I could kill for a smoke. I guess that makes me hypocritical for laughing at the aide for making out cheques to herself. Someone who has survived both lung and throat cancer should really be trying to kick the habit, instead of hiding cigarettes in the heating ducts.

Lillian's being buried next to Chuck. Who is buried next to Dad. Who is not next to Mother, of course. Mother is just across the road, within waving distance. Mind you, I think they were on more intimate terms than that. Ha ha ha.

The geniuses at the group home didn't think Ida should go to the funeral but I made them see reason. Lillian was *Chuck's* wife, for goodness sake. I had to hire a muscle-bound young Neanderthal to transport Ida, who must be close on three hundred pounds these days, and he turned out to be a Baumwohl! I kept my hand on my Camels the entire time.

I can't wait to paste Lillian's obituaries in my scrapbook. All of them mention Chuck.

June 26th

Weiner, Lillian Phyllis

Lillian, wife of Chuck Weiner, the infamous proprietor of Chuck's Restaurant, was best known as the Laurel to her husband's Hardy. Beloved mother of Sarah and Linda, sister of Reginald, Lawrence and Zelda Gestetner. She will be remembered for her wit and zest, her energetic pursuit of beauty and her strong convictions. Donations to the Susan G. Koman Breast Cancer Foundation.

She had a beautiful funeral. Funny, isn't it, how in the old days we went to weddings and bar mitzvahs, and now all we get on the social calendar are funerals and it's just an excuse for a good old cry together anyway. It's like I've always said, either you get older or you don't. Your choice – birthdays or funerals. And they say such nice things about people at their funerals that it makes me sad that I'm going to miss mine by just a few days. Ha ha ha.

I can't help feeling, though, that Lillian doesn't belong next to Chuck. In my heart, I feel that place belongs to me. We raised a family together, him and I, and Lillian never really became a Weiner. No Weiner would dye her hair that nasty shade of red, would fight so hard to stay looking young. It's miraculous to us Weiners that we made it this far, to grey hair and wrinkles.

On the way to the funeral, I asked the driver to park outside our old house. It's been gussied up, and has flowers growing in the yard, something we could never afford – time and money being both in short supply. Hope in their zealousness they don't decide to put a swimming pool in the backyard.

Rosa called me from Berkeley this afternoon, probably guilty about not coming. She told me she loves me. Liar. I think she's after the family photos. She thanked me for my birthday gift, a freshly minted five-dollar bill. I do the best I can for my sisters, cooped up as I am in this so-called Home. Rosa seemed stunned when I asked her to send me a case of Camels, unfiltered.

June 27th

We have no family photos.

Rosa should remember that, since her first photo was taken at her wedding and when the flash went off, she screamed.

I *might* have taken photos, but when I was fourteen, I was introduced to that slick seducer of children, Polio. Every good mother was keeping her kids off the streets – I kept the girls home from school – but Chuck and I had to work. The doctor told me I breathed in a germ as it floated by. If I had breathed out, I would have been okay. Imagine that.

An ambulance came howling through the streets of New Haven and carted me off to Roosevelt Island. Apparently, I yelled the whole way, 'I've got to take care of my sisters! Get your hands off me! Let me go!' so they knew I wasn't dying anytime soon. And I didn't either. All I remember is being in that eight hundred pound yellow coffin for about a year – the iron lung. The girls on either side of me died, their machines still exhaling whoof, whoof, whoof, for hours after they'd already checked out. The nurses put screens around them but it was too late and I'd been looking at their dead faces all night. One of the nurses said, 'Don't worry, deary. They were poor, weak girls, but you're made of steel.' I think she was thinking of the bite marks she'd gotten on her hands, brushing my teeth, but it was true all the same.

I was given a tutor, a weedy little guy with ears as thin and flimsy as a bat's. You could see every beat of his heart in his hot ears. He had been a writer before the Depression and now he tutored people like me. He ended up liking me, that man, and I liked him too, but raising a family is a full time job. Leaving none left over for fripperies.

He was the one who got me interested in the way words can dance together, do the tango and the cha-cha and the waltz. He spoke in rushes between the gaspings of the iron lungs, and their explosions of compressed air form the cadence of all the poems I have ever memorised, every equation, every date in history or geological land form, their music all conducted by a yellow robot hand.

After I could finally breathe on my own and was able to sleep outside the iron lung, my legs had shrivelled up to hard black poles and were just about as easy to walk on. The doctors fixed me up with metal leg braces and canes, and I hopped around, much more a girl of steel than before.

I learned to smoke in that hospital, because everyone was smoking and I hated the smell. Someone had told me that if you smoked a cigarette yourself, the smell wouldn't bother you, and that was true enough. After a while, you can't smell anything, actually.

Or taste it either. I could have lost my taste for life in the sanatorium, but instead it grew till I could feel it in my mouth, full and round and electric as if a plant of the stuff had grown on my tongue, ferned out into my passages, French-kissed parts of my brain that had never been kissed.

I show my legs to everyone, as nowadays you don't see the results of polio much. I took some photos of my legs too – at last, some family photos! – and have them taped above my rocking bed. The camera flash made my skin look an interesting greenish purple when it's really more of a sulphurous yellow, the paint from the iron lung having stealthily leached into my skin as I slept, a secretive tattoo artist.

Hope my efforts are appreciated. There are crazy people out there who don't believe in immunisation.

June 28th

The sun is shining through the window, cooking me at a slow and tolerable simmer. Amazing, the pleasure I take in a moment of sunshine. Good things can happen, even when you're seventy-six, stuck in a wheelchair at the top of a tower, bumming cigarettes from phlebotomists and mortuary directors, and going to the cemetery to see your friends. Now I just have to hope that my aide remembers I'm a person, not a steak.

Anita got fitted for hearing aids today and it's just as I thought. When she was here, she asked me why she needed them.

June 29th
Mother was sick for weeks until she died. Didn't say a word to me or anyone. Right before she died, she grabbed my hand, hard, and said in a fierce whisper, 'Take care of Tully.' That was what she called Ida. Just 'Take care of Tully,' not a hello, goodbye or I love you. At least I heard that. Some of the others never heard her say a single thing their whole lives.

June 30th
Today I had my aide copy a bunch of obituaries and 'Love is ...' cartoons I've been saving for my nieces. It's her punishment for finding my cigarettes again (inside the towel bar).

Those cartoons always make me wonder if our mother loved us.

Or were we like baby mice, anxious, blind, squeaking things that ate the food and soiled the floor, verminous, never part of her world? Was she the kind of person that Rosa could have tapped on the shoulder, touched, gone walking with in that deep, deep silence and come out knowing something, anything, about the person who lived in there?

If anyone could've, it'd be Rosa. She is a good psychologist. She has lived a good life too, no diabetes or polio or cancer or Huntington's. She's never smoked; she had children of her own, all healthy, and a husband who gave her pearls on her twenty-fifth anniversary. She wanted to leave our home here in this town of secrets, and she did. She opened her practice out in Berkeley, California, and left us all open-mouthed, open-handed, an opening in our childish circle into which only sadness could crawl, tail between its legs. That miserable cur has been with us ever since, instead of our hero, our Rosa.

If she were here, I wouldn't be smoking.

That's a lie.

I *would* be smoking, but not in bed.

Oh Lord, just let me outlive my sisters, all except Rosa. She'll know how to bury me.

July 1st

But I'm the expert on burial.

The day Mother died was hot, one of those east-coast thunderstorms miles high, a dirty damburst about to close in over our heads. Fish could have breathed in that air, eels slipped through the muddy flotsam, but Mother, drowning in her own spit, couldn't.

Chuck closed her eyes. We didn't like being in the same room with a dead person, our second one face-to-face, but the truth was, she looked about the same. Peed herself, of course, but she wasn't too fussy about the niceties even on an ordinary day. I swear she was still sweating.

In the three years since Dad had passed on, Mother – despite her silence – had been vital to us. She was the mooring that kept us from being washed away, caught in the strong whirlpool that had as its epicentre the local Hebrew orphanage. We had seen the orphans bobbing by the gate, their heads barely out of water, all trying so hard to swim away from there, bureaucratic seaweed tangled around their bare legs, salt water dripping from their hair, their noses, their eyes.

That night in the heat we dug a hole in the backyard, Chuck and I throwing the ashy dirt to one side, bitter odours rising as the shovels scraped against the willow roots writhing in the earth. Chuck lay her pillow at one end, where he guessed her head would land, and we rolled her in. She didn't weigh much, but she was stiff, as dead people are, awkward to move, and she smelling sweetish. I dropped a sheet down over her, because a blanket seemed unkind in the humidity.

Rosa woke up and heard us out there, shovelling back the stained and bitter earth, and she came and stood on the back stairs, a tiny gibbous moon reflected in each of her eyes. Said Chuck should say kaddish, so he did and we said Amen, which means 'God is the faithful king,' and then we sat there together, making sure with our silence that we would be joined with our mother, that no one would ever tell.

It wasn't hard to pretend she was still alive, lying in her bed. No one noticed her absence, least of all us.

Naturally, there were no obituaries for her either.

July 2nd

Last night, in my sleep, I saw my mother place child after child in the garbage can. When she went away, I took them all out again. They were dirty, so I bathed them. They smiled at me, but I saw them flickering, transparent in my hands. I woke up smelling their sweet soapy skin and needing a cigarette so badly I could cry.

July 3rd

Katzenellenbogen, Francine

Francine Katzenellenbogen, a North Haven–born lottery millionaire who loved cats so much she built a mansion for 20 beloved strays, died on June 30 at her home. She was 51 and may have loved cats rather more than was good for her. Her aunt, Lorraine Katzenellenbogen of Millford, said the cause was a chronic asthma condition aggravated by an strong allergic reaction to cats.

I interviewed Ida's new aide today and she seems honest, or at least a cautious liar. She has a cat and says she'll bring it in for Ida to hold. Ida's mad about cats, their warmth and purring providing a sense that there is something in this world that finds her lovable. Any day now, I'll be cutting out her obituaries and gluing them in my scrapbook and what will they say? What can they say? Even though she's so much like a child, there won't be any sad little poems written by doting parents. I don't want to see her go, can hardly bear the thought of it, but her mind has been gone from us a long time and it'd just be her body catching up.

July 4th

Life for me ain't been no crystal stair.
It's had tacks in it,
And splinters,
And boards torn up,
And places with no carpet on the floor –
Bare.
But all the time
I'se been a-climbin' on ...

The words of Hughes' poem have become an obsessive refrain that I find myself whispering as I am placed on the toilet, as my backside is wiped, as my hair is washed, as Anita shouts her boring stories, as my blood is drawn and sometimes as I write I can hear the words 'I'se been a-climbin' on' drifting up towards me from these pages.

How ironic that today is Independence Day.

I have kept myself going all these years for my sisters and

when they are gone – and they are disappearing before my very eyes – what will happen to me? My silence will protect no one, my concern will save no one. I will be the old lady whose thick yellow toenails daily cut holes in her mismatched socks, whose false teeth dangle from the aide's rear-view mirror, whose clothes are salvaged from those left behind after others' family members clear out their rooms. I will be the old biddy muttering my story, over and over until it's unintelligible, the words thirty syllables long. Kind-hearted strangers will detour around me for fear of being ashamed when they have to escape my mad circle. Every word a knife called lonesome.

What does all this scribbling mean? Why let myself think about it? But I do wonder, sometimes, what my life might have been like if I had fallen in love with Bat Ears and him with me? If my own life had come before the lives of my siblings? What if I'd had my own children or never learned to smoke, or breathed out instead of in when Old Man Polio walked by? What if I'd become a writer or a trapeze artist or a dyke? What if my sisters and I had become a famous singing and dancing troupe? The CHARMING Sisters, singing at all the Catskill hotspots, wearing pasties with tassels and tiaras in their hair. Bunk. If my grandmother had had wheels she'd have been a train. These are foolish lies. The truth is, we had all the essentials. I lied, too, about not wanting my nieces to read this diary. I want them to know that, despite everything, we had companionship and understanding and new shoes with all the buttons. We had love.

This is What I Want; This is What I Don't Want

A city like any city. A subway too. You can lose everything on these streets. When people walk past, their shoes are eight inches from my head; my pillow is my older sister's arm. She is ten. The piss on her clothes is frozen. What would you be willing to lose if there was something you weren't willing to lose? We beg. Two dollars is enough for a bottle of paint. It's cheaper than food and it lasts all day and you never get hungry. Plastic bags for the paint are free in the garbage. If you get paint on your pants, the soup kitchen won't let you in. 'Drug addict,' the Soup Lady says when she hits me. I told her I am a boy but she hits me anyway.

This is what we want: To tell you a story so you'll give us some money.

This is what we don't want: Pity.

My mind thinks, all the time, of death. The tiles under my cheek are cold and hard. Grit cuts into my skin. There are lice crawling up my back. I am warmer than the tiles. The scream of the trains is making us deaf. I do have a daddy. I do have a mummy. I came to my sister's room two years ago, broke the window and stole her away. She wanted to go. Men tremble with desire. Now, we beg.

Above the subway station is a flag with a harp on it. People, they say, are coming from Ireland to play like the angels in heaven. I am no angel. My sister though. I wash my hands in the cold coffee the man from the café throws out and it stains my skin. They beat me here. They beat my sister. They beat the others. They say we steal. We steal cartons to sleep on. We steal empty bottles to drink from. We steal chunks of concrete to protect ourselves. We steal air to breathe. Yes we steal.

This is the subway station. Upstairs, there is grass and wind. Upstairs is the sun. We live downstairs. My sister is psychotic. That's what the others say. She smiles a lot. She cries. It's hard for her to walk. I call her Nose. Hers is small, like a dog's. Her ears are small too and down by her chin. I call her a boy's name but they still cane her when she cries. Her thumbs are small. Her tongue sticks out. I'll break the face of anyone who touches her. In winter, we coat each other, first me on her back, then her on mine. In summer, she gives me a rubber ball to lick. It tastes like shoes.

This is what we want: To get into the shelter.

This is what we don't want: To go back home.

But this is what happens: The cops come at night and lock the gates of the train station. They put us in two trucks. One truck leaves and I never see those kids again. The Fancy Lady asks my sister where she's from and what is her name and why isn't she talking and when I tell her my sister can't speak, the Fancy Lady tells me to shut up until it's my turn. She tells me to butt out my cigarette. She tells me to go wash my hands. She gives me a T-shirt and tells me that girls cover their chests, but I tell her I am no girl and I put the shirt on my head and tie it under my chin and it's a scarf.

This is what I want: Paper.

This is what I don't want: Kindness.

The Man With the Square Beard brings us back to the house of the mother and the father and he asks them if they want us. They shake their heads. 'Go fuck yourselves!' I shout. 'I don't know these people! Who are they?' I take the chunk of concrete from my pocket. They put on their fear faces. I slash the chunk against my arm and blood, blood, blood on their bed. This house is made of packing crates, cabbages grow in the refrigerator.

I am deaf from the trains. My sister is not deaf, but she does not speak. She is smiling now. She wants to hug these people. They pat her head. Bald, we are twins. She is ten. I am eight. In the station, they beat us for even having a mother and a father. 'Human!' they spit. 'Face first out of an ass. That's nothing to be proud of!' But they must have parents too. They must. My sister finds a stray dog and rocks it in her arms and hums. Dogs fuck. Dogs have babies. Dogs eat their babies. I can sleep through having my hair cut with a knife.

The mother wears a man's pyjama top and watches us to see that we don't steal her bread. She glued the labels on bottles of nail polish until she didn't anymore. One bottle of vodka costs more than ten loaves of bread. She is so thin that the bones in her neck have skin bridges between them. 'You've never loved me,' she says. 'It's you leaving me.' There is a plastic clock shaped like a cat. Tick tock. 'They are crazy,' she says. 'That one's a Mongoloid,' she says. 'What did they tell you?' she says. 'She's still a virgin,' the father says. 'I'm telling the truth,' he says. 'I bathed her,' he says. 'So I know.'

This is what I want: To be good.

This is what I don't want: Ever to leave my sister.

When it rains, dogs come and lick the water out of the cracks in the concrete. The buildings are grey. They have red doors. I'm not really from here. I am from pine trees and chickens and pink horses. I have another house. I have another country. I have another mother. I don't want to die.

When it is very bad, I put paint in a bag for my sister, and I put her face down in the bag and I squeeze the plastic and she breathes and then I breathe and then we both go to visit our other country. Our other brothers and sisters are in school. Everyone has just had lunch. They have gravy on their chins and white underwear and tricycles with bells. The silver paint in the bag makes my sister a beard, her head falls back, she moans, there is no now but this now, this pine tree farm place with sudden buses roaring through it. Watch out for the buses. They are real.

Your hand has a map of roads on it, white roads, and when you are lost all you need to do is look at the back of your hand. It's all there. Some of the others forget and get lost. Some of the others are hit by buses. Some of the others go to sleep and get cold and stiff and are taken away by the garbage collectors. Read the map. Don't forget. There are places you can never go.

My sister gave me a tennis ball once. And once she gave me a can of Coke. And once she found a bandaid for my face when it was broken. Her arm is my pillow and my head is hers. She has the breasters now and I get her bigger clothes, no one will see. To be noticed, is death. To be weak, is death. To be slow, is death. To be girl, is death. We are not girl.

She pisses herself in the street. In the winter, it freezes us together as we sleep. I want to be good. I want to draw a picture to make her happy. I want to write her name on it so I can find her if I go away. I pat her face as she sleeps and this she likes. What is her name?

Fancy Lady catches me in the streets on a day when there has been no food. She says I can learn and she shows me things. She says another mother will take me but only me. She shows me the shelter and it is quiet there and clean. No trains. She feeds me and then I sleep. Where is my sister? Get my sister. Fancy Lady only shrugs.

There is that look that people have when they are holding something back.

There is another look when they are lying.

So I run out of the Fancy Lady's window and my sister is already asleep on the cartons in the subway station when I get back, her face full of salt. 'I'm home,' I say. 'I won't go,' I say. 'Don't cry,' is what I say.

When we beg, she opens her mouth and puts out her hands. Money, only sometimes, falls in. She is afraid of water, afraid of birds, afraid of the man near the doors with his accordion and his grey teeth. She smells the money and wrinkles her nose. Nose is my name for her. Not girl name. 'Aaaaaah,' she says, sun on her face. Rain, when it comes, sends her screaming to hide in the broken bottles. Her scream is a sound like a train turning a corner and I hold my hands over her ears until she stops. She is afraid of her screams. A finger on her lip is her sign for me because I bring her food. Paint forgets us about food. We are so thin. She would be leaves in November if they took me away. She can't learn. They don't want her at the shelter. No mother will love her except for me. I've asked.

This is what I want.
    This is what I don't want.

Undesirable

Masha thought it was because she'd had cancer that nobody wanted to marry her. The cancer had been an impure stain that spread through her body, tainting it forever. It was hard enough, going back to seminary two years after her friends had already graduated, but then came the slow and brutal torture of seeing even these younger girls getting engaged, then married and eventually blurting out babies. At the never-ending weddings, no eligible young men peeped into the women's section and let their eyes rest on her. The matchmaker never called. Slowly, like a nail tearing through her flesh, all sixty of her classmates were married off until she was the last one remaining. Undesirable.

'They're afraid of our family now,' said her father. 'First your mother and then you.' Seeing her stricken face, he patted her hand. 'At least you're still alive.'

It was no comfort at all.

She felt the stain eating at her in the morning when she woke and washed her hands, watching the water to see if it changed colour after contact with her skin. What colour is impurity? Is it brown? Or black? Or a sickly yellow-green? She washed her hands a second time and a third. She scrubbed at the humid places on her body that exuded an odour of fermentation, and she checked the colour of the run-off under the fluorescent strip. The stain was there. She could see it.

'You're obsessed,' said her father, the night he caught her

examining her bathwater under a microscope she'd lugged home from work. 'Obsessed. You know the cancer's gone. There's nothing left.'

Which felt true. She was a husk. The chemotherapy had burnt out her organs, leaving nothing behind. It had tattooed the inside of her skin with a pharmacological warning. Unclean.

On the day before Yom Kippur, when many women and girls queued up to use the ritual baths on Albany Avenue, she stood in the line three times just to feel, for a moment, the purifying water close over her head like a shroud, sealing her off from contamination. But the second her face broke the mirrored surface, she saw again the jostling line of women in terrycloth robes edging away from her, trading places so they wouldn't have to enter the water directly after the damaged girl. And echoing down the tiled corridors came the whispers, 'Such horrifying scars. She'll never get married.'

Of all the indignities, this was the worst. Crown Heights was a community that believed in marriage, that announced marriages and births the way the secular world announced a rise in the Dow Jones Industrial Average.

'You might,' said the matchmaker for special cases, 'Try finding someone from overseas, someone who hasn't heard of your misfortune. Maybe,' she cleared her throat, 'It would be better to look for a newcomer to Judaism.'

Masha's skin prickled. The hairs on her arms stood up.

'A convert?' she whispered, disbelieving.

'Of course not,' laughed the matchmaker, 'No. I was only suggesting a Baal Teshuvah, someone who didn't grow up religious.'

This idea repelled Masha and she couldn't understand why. A Baal Teshuvah, after all, might be kind, educated, tolerant.

He wouldn't come with a mother who was pregnant at their wedding, probably wouldn't have sixty-seven nieces and nephews and might even have a car. It would be relatively easy to hide her history from someone who hadn't grown up in Brooklyn. He wouldn't know a thing until she proved unable to have children.

One day, as she passed the ritual baths on her way to purchase a pound of rugelach from the bakery, she realised what it was that was so upsetting about marrying a Baal Teshuva. He too would have a stain, the taint of an impure birth that could never be erased. She rushed into the bakery and begged the old Hungarian woman behind the counter if she could use the bathroom. She needed to wash her hands. They felt as if tiny fungi were erupting in their life lines, slimy and vigorous in a way that she had previously associated with maggots. 'Go right ahead, darling,' said the crone. 'You don't look too good.'

That night, however, the matchmaker called with a suggestion, a Baal Teshuva boy from Long Island, and Masha's father seemed eager to hear about him, the first boy suggested in six years. 'Up and coming!' he repeated, waggling his eyebrows in Masha's direction. 'Not from a divorced family!' But then he turned from Masha and tugged at his beard. 'College? I don't know. He wasn't involved in anything, you say? Do you have proof?'

College! The floor under Masha's feet tilted and edged her towards the fireplace. Everyone knew that people who went to college were apostates, ruined absolutely. The gas jet hissed. Upstairs, the tenant's children rode their tricycles down the long hallway, louder and louder, faster and faster, until they crashed into the wall with a sound like a sixteen-pound bowling ball knocking down every single pin at the end of the alley. She felt herself totter, bowled over by this unknown assailant's life.

'Do we have a choice?' her father was saying, and then he hung up and turned to her with a watery smile. 'Looks like you're going to be meeting a boy, missy my Lou.' A fine something snapped inside her to hear her father call her by that pet name. He'd last used it when she was a girl of four or five, sitting in the hospital waiting room with him, both of them too shattered to go in and see what the surgeons had left of her mother. It was the name he used when she needed to be brave and put on a smiling face. 'He's very clever,' said her father and she put her head against his chest and began to cry. 'You never know. He might turn out to be charming.'

They met several nights later in her dining room and she saw instantly that he was quite poor. He wore a polyester suit and one of those shirts that never looked ironed and never looked white. Beyond that she couldn't go. She was shy, much too shy to look at his face, but his fingernails were clean and each one had a beautiful mauvish moon rising in it. She was pleased that she had bought a new dress if only because he might be tempted by money, some people were, and the dress had cost her a week's wages. It was an olive and mustard–coloured wool with acanthus leaves winding over it, and she traced the leaves on her lap as he spoke.

'You seem very quiet,' he said. 'Is everything all right?'

She couldn't lose this chance. It might not be repeated. All right. It wouldn't be repeated.

'I'm just listening. I'm a good listener.' She blushed to praise herself. Was she a good listener? She didn't know. She didn't have any friends who'd tell her.

At one point, he excused himself to use to the bathroom and

she ran after him.

'Oh no! I forgot,' she lied. 'The bathroom's not working.' She was fairly sure that her father earlier flushed the toilet and wondered if the young man had noticed. All her bottles of medicine were still lined up on the glass shelf below the mirror. Each one labelled with her accusation of a name. A man who'd gone to college would know what they meant.

'Perhaps we'd better say goodnight.'

He stared at her, at her expensive shoes, her new haircut, her mother's pearls. She'd tried too hard. She knew it now. Or maybe he was just imagining her using a chamber-pot, her skirts hiked up to her thighs.

'All right,' he said.

They parted without exchanging a handshake, a telephone number or a smile. For a Baal Teshuva, he knew a lot of their customs. The extreme physical separation of the sexes until after marriage, even an accidental bumping of shoes under a table completely taboo and cause for embarrassment.

'Well?' said her father. 'Tolerable?'

She took out her prayer book and, kissing it, began to say the evening devotions.

'I don't know,' she said. 'What do I know about that kind of thing? I've never even had a brother.'

'What about me?'

'It's not the same.'

'What?' he said, laughing. 'I'm not young and handsome anymore?' He stroked his snow-white beard. It had changed colour overnight when he heard his young wife's diagnosis. 'Even though you've kept yourself pure all these years, after you get married, all that drops aside. You have to be physically attracted.'

'Gross,' she said, shuddering.

'It's not that bad,' he said, and she knew he was thinking about her mother. After all his loss, he deserved some happiness. She resolved to try harder if the boy wanted another meeting, to think up something interesting to say in advance. At least to look high enough up his chest to see the colour of his beard.

They met in her dining room the next time also, and she saw he had a pale, bullet-shaped head and eyes the colour of toothpaste. He brought her a pad of artist paper which she left lying on the table and didn't touch. Presents were strictly forbidden before an engagement. Surely *someone* had told him? She tried not to wince every time he inserted a hard English O into the softer Hebrew words, every time he placed the accent on the wrong syllable. He sounded raw. New to things. He still had bright brass buttons on his jacket. He probably hadn't noticed that it wasn't the style in Hassidic circles.

'What's that?' she asked, flustered, when she noticed him staring at her in puzzlement. 'Did you ask me a question?'

'You weren't listening,' he said, flatly.

'Oh! But I was!' she said, leaning forward, picturing her father's white beard. 'Truly. You're very interesting to talk to.'

She'd gone too far. He blushed and she blushed and then he said, 'I like you too.'

These words weren't part of the script. Matches were utterly impersonal. Compliments were never paid, certainly in all the stories she'd heard of arranged marriages, no one had ever mentioned a boy openly stating that he liked a girl.

'Excuse me,' she said, standing. She held herself to a walk until she turned into the corridor leading to the bathroom. Then she ran, high heels skidding on the wooden boards and locked herself safely away from that maniac. She washed her hands and face and thought of what to do. The word *abomination* popped into her head, unbidden.

Did he really like her? Or did he simply covet the prestige of marrying into an old Hassidic family? And who was she to complain anyway? She'd agreed to meet someone grossly unsuitable simply because there was no one else, no other possibilities.

'Are you all right?' he asked from right outside the bathroom door. 'Should I go away? Did I say something wrong?' He rattled the doorknob. 'Can I come in?' Was this the way things were done in the secular world? Did boys, with impecunity, enter the bathroom while a girl was inside?

'No!' she shouted. 'I'm fine. I'll be out soon.'

She waited to hear his footsteps going modestly away but apparently he'd never heard of the idea that a boy shouldn't witness a girl leaving the bathroom. Baal Teshuva, she thought bitterly.

When she came out, he rushed at her. She thought he might actually touch her, put his hand on her skin, and she cringed back against the dimpled glass in the bathroom door.

'You've been crying,' he said. 'Please forgive me.'

'No. Not at all. I just washed my face. It's nothing.'

He was almost standing on her toes, much nearer to her than even her father allowed himself.

'Are you sure you're okay?'

She could tell he was used to physically calming his companions. He was close enough to put his arm around her, seemed to be twitching with the urge to hug her back into equanimity.

'Yes,' she said and he stepped back.

A fungal forest had erupted on her palms but it was too late to return to the bathroom and scrub it off.

'Do you want to listen to some music? What have you got?'

Music, she'd been told, aroused unsuitable passions. It wasn't exactly a kosher choice for a meeting between a boy and a girl.

'Uh,' she said. 'Uh ...' Surely he wouldn't be interested in her father's collection of early cantorial recordings. 'I think ... my father ...' She couldn't get out a single intelligent sentence. Any second, this last-moment reprieve would be out the door like a shot, never to return. 'She's a cretin, I think,' he'd tell his friends. 'Brain damaged.'

'Ah,' said the boy. Not such a boy really, a man with a full beard. 'Listening to music isn't done on a date.' She flinched to hear their pathetic blundering from misstep to misstep described as a date. 'Tell me next time. I'm such an idiot.' He almost touched her hand but pulled back at the last minute. 'We'll just talk.'

In the end, to make him comfortable, she walked over to the table and picked up the Arches paper.

'How did you know that I like to draw?' she asked, and he pointed at the paintings on the wall, framed in heavy carved walnut. 'I noticed them last time. They're very good. I can't believe no one told me how talented you are.' He looked right at her then, and smiled.

'I'd like to meet you again,' he said. 'You're very unusual.'

When her father came into her room later, to ask about the meeting, she left out the bathroom fiasco and how uncomfortable she had felt standing next to Yitzchak. She lied when her father asked her if she thought the boy would want to meet a third time. The third time would mean a marriage proposal.

'I don't know,' she said, using the traditional reply. 'We'll have to wait and see what the matchmaker says.' She said this knowing that Yitzchak wanted to meet her again, had said that she was very unusual. She imagined she was protecting her father's feelings by not revealing the ways in which the boy was unfamiliar with their culture, his crude comfort with other, more licentious forms of conduct. Her father would be appalled, she thought. She was appalled.

Before the third meeting, the matchmaker called and told them that Yitzchak wanted to take her out to a restaurant, unaccompanied, in his car. Her father protested.

'It's not done. It's not our way,' he said, pulling the telephone into the closet under the stairs and shutting the door. She could still hear his voice. 'I can't allow it. Absolutely not.' But then his voice got quieter and quieter and she only heard him sigh, once.

'He wants to take you to a restaurant,' he said when he came out of the closet, brushing cobwebs from his beard. And when she began to protest, he laid his dear, liver-spotted old hand on her arm and said, 'Yitzchak told the matchmaker that if you refuse, he's not interested in continuing. I'm sorry, Masha.'

So they met outside her house that third time and drove to a restaurant in another neighbourhood and while they were there, sometime after the soup but before the fortune cookies, Yitzchak asked her if she wanted to get married.

'Yes,' she said, trying to still the violent shaking of her voice and her hands and her thighs. The ground shifted. A volcano exploded through her.

'Fantastic,' said Yitzchak, like a normal human being, and then, not like a normal human being, he climbed onto the seat of his chair and began to sing in a loud, slightly off-key falsetto, 'Wonder of wonders, Miracle of miracles, God took a tailor by the hand. Turned him around and – miracle of miracles – led him to the Promised Land.' As Yitzchak sang these last words, he pointed at her and smiled. He kept on singing and the entire restaurant, about sixty Hassidic Jews, turned around and stared at him in silence.

She felt as if she'd been nailed to her chair and run through with a piece of barbed wire. Every Jew in the room looked in her direction, frowning. No little old lady emerged from the kitchen, clapping her hands and saying, 'How romantic!' It was completely off the charts.

What kind of girl, she could see them thinking, would go out with a boy who sang non-Jewish love songs to her in public places? She'd never heard the song before but recognised it as sappy and sentimental, an unabashed love song. She knew when she was an ancient and toothless old hag holed up in a nursing home somewhere near Sheep's Head Bay she'd be able to remember the tune. All of it carved into her protesting flesh.

Yitzchak jumped off the chair, flushed and laughing. 'I'm getting married,' he said, turning to the frigid crowd, and hitting himself in the chest. 'I'm so lucky! She's agreed to marry me!'

There were a few muttered mazel tovs and the gradual return of restaurant noise: the click of spoons against teeth, the gluck of overhasty swallowings, the susurration of napkins wiping grease from chins.

'Come on,' he said, holding out his hand to her, as if he was asking her to dance, and then abruptly changing the forbidden motion into a request for the bill. 'Let's go tell your Dad.'

She hated it when he called her father 'dad'. That was how

non-Jews spoke. Without respect. He didn't seem to notice that she was a puddle of embarrassment and dislike. He seemed to think he'd done something cute. It was enough to make her cry.

Her father, when they told him, was euphoric. 'Thank God!' he said, over and over again. 'At last!' She was, after all, twenty-six, a good six years older than the average bride. And at this, she put aside the sense she'd had at the restaurant that something was dreadfully, awfully wrong and tried, instead, to revel in the look of joy on her father's face.

But that night, remembering the restaurant, she felt disgust build up in her throat, a new and unfamiliar filth throttling her and she crept into her father's room and woke him up.

'We should tell him.'

'Absolutely not,' said her father, sitting up and turning on the light.

'It's false pretences. We learned that it's not a real marriage if you hide an important detail. It's deception.'

'If you tell him,' said her father, staring at her flat chest, 'He'll never marry you.'

This, she knew, was true. She had been, for many years, an undesirable match.

'It just doesn't seem right somehow.'

'What isn't right is that both your mother and you got breast cancer at twenty. How is that right? Answer me that. What isn't right is that some bastard surgeon hacked off your breasts and tossed them in an incinerator to burn like the six million. Wouldn't even let me bury them properly in a Jewish cemetery. How is this right? And because of it, your life is ruined. How is this right?'

Masha's arms had moved up to cover her chest.

Her father had never said anything even remotely like this before. He sighed. 'Don't say anything,' he said.

Slightly over a week before the wedding, Yitzchak called to speak to her father.

'He's not in,' she said. 'He's gone to the airport to pick up my grandmother.'

'How long will he be gone?'

'I don't know. You could try back in an hour or two.' She was more used to talking to him, but still couldn't think of anything to say on the telephone.

Within a few minutes, the doorbell rang. It was Yitzchak.

'Hello,' she said, blushing. He knew her father wasn't home. It was grossly inappropriate to visit.

'I have to talk to you about something important,' he said, edging forwards, and her bowels shrivelled. Some busybody had finally told him about his new bride. 'Can I come in?' Not really. Not according to the ancient laws of privacy between men and women. She hesitated but then opened the door wider. She didn't want the neighbours to overhear what he had to say.

'Come,' she said, leading him into the living room. She didn't sit down and neither did he. It seemed too familiar. They'd only met each other once or twice after the engagement. Together, they leaned on the mantle over the gas fire. Strangers after five meetings.

'You know how you asked me if I was wild in college?' he asked, as usual standing far too close. She'd wanted to know if he'd taken drugs, dyed his hair purple, been a member of some scary militant group, streaked naked across campus, worst of all, done things, forbidden things with girls, but being unable to articulate any of these, had simply asked if he was wild. 'No,' he'd said then. 'I'm not that kind of boy.'

But now she saw how red his ears were, reflected in the large gilded mirror over the mantle. 'Yes,' she said. 'I did ask that.'

'I want you to know the truth about me before we're married,' he said. He wiped a shaking hand over his face where a dozen little pearls of sweat shone. 'I told a lie before and that's no way to start a relationship. I did drugs,' he said. 'I tried them all. I got drunk every Friday night and threw up in the pricker bushes near my fraternity house. I still smoke a joint every Purim.' She had no idea what he meant, but nodded to encourage him. 'I've ...' He looked at her and looked away, a carmine bloom spreading down into the open neck of his shirt. 'I've had girlfriends. A lot of girlfriends.' She'd suspected as much. 'I've *known* them,' he said, emphasising the biblical even in this. 'I'm not pure like you,' he said. 'You are so innocent. I've never met anyone like you. I can't believe I'll be married to you in a week. Do you still want to get married to me after hearing this stuff?'

She could feel the air boiling off him, sweetish with the smell of the spray starch he used. His face seemed to waver in the rising miasma. Her own face was burning. She could see it in the mirror, the exact colour of a crushed cherry. Had he just confessed that he'd had sex with other girls? She thought that's what he'd intended to say.

'I don't care about those other girls,' he said now. 'I only want you. Please,' he said, putting out his hand. 'Let me touch you, just once, before we are married.'

She stared at his hand, alone there in the hell between them.

He wanted her. He said so himself. He *desired* her.

'I have something to tell you too,' she said. Her fingers twitched. Soon they would move.

His hand seemed to glow. The purple moons rising, rising, always rising.

Disposable

Well, now, I sure do feel like everyone's looking at me, stuck here on this plastic chair together with the gobs of gum, hard as life. Reckon they think I'm something off of a postcard, eyeballing my bonnet, my black shoes that I got for fifty cents from Goodwill and they wadn't hardly used at all. I'd never sit myself down in a place like this if I had any kind of choice. Choice. Now that'd be nice.

See. I'm here for my littlest one, Alvin, he's been ailing for a whiles now, just sitting here against me, limp as a week-old stick of celery, eyes like mine so much, blue that's almost white, but his don't seem to see much all of anything nowadays. Light's always bothering him and making his eyes just run with the water. They give him some kind of treatment, medicine that made some bit of skin inside of his eyeballs roll up like one of them shades. Reckon they must have known it might do that, but I'm not complaining.

Something bad comes over me sitting here, like ants crawling over my parts, a-nibbling at me, trying to make me squirm. I never would. Squirm, that is. Give them English folk something more to look at. Ha! Reckon they'll be thinking I turned into a stone or a tree or a post. But I stick a finger up under my bonnet, kind of without thinking, when that little kid with no hair asks her mam, 'Why that lady got a bucket on her head?' Her mam doesn't look my way, but I know the kid meant me, and her mam is looking all kinds of red and telling it how Amish are old-fashioned and like to wear buckets on their heads and she looks around the waiting room at this, and all the folks nod except me, because I'm this tree getting gnawed on by ants. I'd like to touch my bald spot again, really I would, but instead I try to reason whether the driver is going to be drunk when he picks us up. Or not.

The lady that they got cleaning in here pushes this bucket of scummy water in the door with her mop, and she's just pushing the dirt around, spreading it out even like, as if it's wax. She bangs the mop up against the wall so there's a real nasty rim of gunk there, a ring in this bathtub of a room. Takes the dust can and dumps it after she's mopped around and a big puff of dust and rotting tissues floats up and settles on the damp floor. I'm not complaining. Hope it don't sound like I am. I wouldn't do that. No ways.

Ha! See that? What'd I tell you. Fella over there is practically wetting his britches. He sees Amish people! In the cancer clinic! Up to Rochester! He's busting to run off and tell his sweetie. It'll take a couple more minutes and then he'll remember he's got this disposable camera in his backpack, and his hand will creep on over to get it, and he'll be figuring how he can snap a picture without me noticing.

I get the itch in the worst kind of way and my finger seems to slide by itself in under my bonnet and touch this little bald spot I have under there. You can't see it. It's under my cap, on the top there, where the pin goes. After a while us ladies get a bald spot from the pin rubbing at the place. I noticed it a ways back and sometimes I like to touch it. Kind of run my finger over it. So I touch it again.

Sitting here so long with nothing at all to do just seems like a bad waste of time. Every nurse or cleaning lady walks in here, I reckon it's going to be us they're calling. Never is, and the clock has just about stopped on the wall. Seems like about a minute between each tick and the English folk just a-staring the whole time at me. Just sit and sit and sit. Never move a single speck. Wooden post.

Well, hey, the nurse just come and called my boy's name, 'Herschberger ... Alvin Herschberger, step right through here please,' and I call out softly, 'I think that'd be us.' And that's when she's sees me getting up, lifting poor Alvin, and her eyes open the tiniest bit and you can bet she's thinking, 'Now I seed it all.'

But I just march up there, Alvin in my arms, and I don't even blink when I hear the flashbulb pop. It's a temptation to reach over and squash that man flat, but that'd only be good for about a second or two. Reckon he'll be feeling a mite bad when he picks up them photos and sees my boy's empty eyes. Reckon he'll wish he hadn't a done it then.

Never Eat Crow

She was three, maybe four, when they sold her. Someone bent down and put their lips on her forehead and that was goodbye. A fence all made from sticks, a willow tree, a geranium growing in a bucket. Grass mown by a horse pulling a cutter bar.

The second step from the top was always damp. Dew fell on the bleached wood from the lip of the tin roof and on summer mornings, when Soile sat there, her bare feet cringed from the cold. Cold is a killer. She was the cleaning lady; on this island, this year, every one of the visiting people used her. They said she never stole, but she did. Not small things. Large. Mattresses. Lamps. A rocking chair, a family portrait, a painted Norwegian chest that she'd carried away on her back as the owners sat picnicking under the birches, her hand hooked through one of the heavy iron handles, her head almost touching her knees.

She wore the front of her black hair parted and tied into braids, and the back covered with a bit of cloth shattered from use. Ears looked like dried apricots to her, tart and delicious. This island, so small and green and singing with life in the Finnish summer, was barely a hunch of snow sticking out of the frozen sea in winter. Now, she came each week with that year's dog, Hamlet, and a sled. A long-haired dog can keep you from freezing. Hamlet, besides, had blue eyes.

The whiteness is blinding. Nothing else exists. The snow

over the ice melts in the momentary midday sun and refreezes into a crust. Walking, she broke through with each step, a push, a crack, a fall into solidity. Again and again. All the way from Rymättylä. The summer people paid her poorly in the winter, but better than they knew.

No one came except hunters. Once, twice a day, a shot. Perhaps the hunters. Perhaps the ice. During storms, the hiss of ice razoring the walls of the cabins. Where did all that summer go? Sometimes seeds or dragonflies or autumn leaves were trapped in the ice. The ice breathes. Melt, on the surface, slicks back and forth with each breath. Watch the early larvae swimming and you will see.

She, Soile, comes this morning, her paw on another girl's arm.

'Are you sure it's all right?' says the chattering nervousness.

'Which house to stay in?'

One cabin has antlers piled up to the roofline, invisible against the snow except for where they have mouldered.

'Don't they mind?'

Soile holds up the ring of keys. Four keys. 'Which?'

They met in summer on a different island in the archipelago, where Soile had gone to sell a three-hundred year old mirror and to eat crayfish. Wasps built houses like lotus pods under the wide eaves of the café. She thought she'd seen the girl, Lena, before but, try as she might, no memory came forth.

'What are you?' she said, and Lena, giggling, said nineteen years old, one hundred and sixty-five centimetres tall, plump, carbon-based naughty girl.

'Naughty?' Soile said, her teeth showing, and the girl, under the table, pushed her foot forward and touched Soile's bare toes.

The meadows were filled with tiny yellow butterflies that summer, absolutely filled. Upon closer examination, they have pink legs, and hairy. Chickens and roosters crawk under all verandas, too many, too many. By the end of the summer there will be fewer. The dog and she will be rounder. Feathers can be stuffed into plastic grocery bags and pushed between a sweater and a shirt, for warmth, come winter. Chicken fat, rubbed on the face and ears, protects against frostbite. Almost nothing better than the cold slip of fresh-laid egg raw in the throat, the sweet smooth shell kissed between the lips. Pleasure feels like raw egg. Walk too fast through the marshy places and mud will splatter up your calves and thighs. Smells of mushrooms, rotten wood, shit.

She falls in love with fat. One bite and she knows if it will be worth her while to digest. Sweet sweet fat, shining and soft and slippery, bubbles of winter joy. Chew or spit when once you knew. Owls look big, but there's only a bare handful of greasy meat under all that fluff. Never eat crow if you value your life.

On the old maps, she'd been told it said 'No Man's Land' ... she liked the sound of that, wanted it tattooed across her chest, but was afraid of the pain and her own blood and the no-going-backness. She'd never met a man who seemed anything more than the most tepid of lap dogs but she hated to rule out possibilities. About the unknown, the other thing it said on old maps was, 'Here be dragons.'

Fir wood, under your feet, feels gritty. Pine feels hot. Walnut is cool and smoky. Maple needs sex and demands it now. She liked linoleum for the way it sold itself cheaply and didn't try to worm its way into your life. Linoleum wore latex hotpants. Linoleum had pink hair and 'No Man's Land' tattooed across its chest. Carpet wore fake pearls but said they were real. Soile always wore men's shirts from the thrift store and a huge floral skirt, so her body was divided above from below, at the line where the shirt ended and the skirt began. She wore an apron too, with pockets cut from old jeans and a loop for her hammer at the hip.

You have no idea what damage you can do to someone's face with a hammer.

When it's forty below, you can sit in a hospital emergency room, and pretend to be waiting for someone. Police on night duty are brought in, with large chunks of their buttocks and noses lost to frostbite. If they wear those gloves that stop at the knuckles so they can smoke, they come in missing fingers. The public library is also a good spot, but they'll ask you to leave if you smell bad. Bathe in the sea even in winter. That's how steel is made strong. By plunging it into cold water. Scrub with sand. Disturbing the patrons, the library says. You can get on the train and just not get off again for days, until you need to eat. A big dog is like owning a fur coat.

Behind the bakery and the fish shop and the grocery are dumpsters full of perfectly good food if you don't mind the food that isn't perfectly good anymore that's in there too. And rats. And used diapers. And needles from the junkies that no matter which way you climb in will always poke you in the bum. Rats are good eating when they are small, especially the tails.

The gay centre in downtown Turku serves a hot lunch on

Mondays because the bakeries and the fish shops and the groceries are all closed on Sundays and the dumpsters are emptied on Saturdays and there's a lot of street kids will eat there and say they are queer just to get food, the liars. She'd like to put the claw of the hammer right into the sockets of their eyes for taking her food. They call her Cat, which is all wrong. She doesn't call them anything. The whiteness is blinding. Nothing else exists. Sometimes she hears the zhring of summer crickets in her head all winter.

Her hands are thick and brown and dirty. Work hands. Her thumbs stop at the first joint and don't have nails. Someone forgot to teach her how to talk right. She makes mistakes like saying, 'What are you?' instead of 'What is your name?' She can drink four litres of milk at one time and only throws up if she bends over. The girl, Lena, is from the mainland. She is going to university. She is pretty and wears a parka that you couldn't freeze in and drives a car and has a plastic card that gives her money whenever she wants it and she smells like Lily-of-the-Valley. She told Soile that when Soile sniffed her neck. 'Lily-of-the-Valley,' she said.

They go into one house after another. Mrs Pekkonen hired Soile right off the street, dog and all, to clean her cabin. She believed that, given decent work and good wages, Soile was reclaimable. On Mrs Pekkonen's Steinway piano, Soile pecked out four bars of Pachelbel's 'Canon'. 'Taught myself,' she says. Mrs Pekkonen patted her on the head.

'Do you have children?' she asks. Soile looks like an old thirty. She thinks she might be fourteen. Or nine. Those are nice numbers.

Then came 'Chopsticks', 'Für Elise', 'Twinkle Twinkle', 'Killing Me Softly'.

The weather turned cold and Mrs Pekkonen went back to Helsinki in her Vulva.

'Check up on the cabin, will you?' she asked. Fifty markka for checking up. And a family portrait. And a Turkish carpet that wore real pearls.

Swings half-buried, the chains driving down into snow. Clear the snow and you can sit with Lena on your lap and swing and swing and swing and not let her go even though she is screaming because it is too high and too long and your fingers are too tight and the frame is shaking and coming up out of the snow. Rust from the chains reddens her hands.

If you wrap your feet in newspapers and then rags and then plastic bags and then duct tape them closed and then put on the extra large gum boots you found at the cabin nearest the dock, your feet will not get cold or wet and you won't lose any more toes. If she loved me, she wouldn't scream. Duct tape hurts like hell when you put it on lips. A chain about the neck is just as swift.

Soile lights the stove with the kindling stacked on the shelves nearby. Never use the leather ones because they stink. The ones with photographs burn green and slow. This is the last house with any kindling left. These are the last pieces of kindling. Crimpling the papers lets the fire eat air.

Hamlet can sniff out good things to eat and he himself will make good eating. She has eaten her other winter coats, all of them larger, fatter dogs she stole from unattended yards or tied up outside shops. Dogs long in loin and rump. Feel for fat where bone lives just under skin. The spine, the ribs. Feel for muscle with two hands around the thigh. Fat is soft and pressable, muscle firm and round, bone is hard.

They never growl or bite or slink away. She runs at them on all four paws, the hair at the nape of her neck bristling. She makes a noise high-pitched and insistent called Doomsday Dog that makes them shiver and pee on their own feet. She bites their tender jowls under the jaw. They know she can and will rip out their throats. Her mouth smells of blood. Wolf-killer. She is not she, to them. In the denim pockets of her apron she keeps raw liver.

Soile examines Lena's ears in the kitchen of the furthest house and pushes her back against the counter. She bites Lena's lip hard and draws blood. There is a leaf that can stop bleeding. It's cottony inside. Crushed mullein takes away the itch of nettles. Lena uncertain. Wipes the blood from her mouth with the back of her hand. Tries to stand. Sweating. The fire is much too hot.

'Whose house is this?' she asks, but Soile leans in and sucks the wound, sucks her lip, fumbles with Lena's zipper. Small flakes of burning paper escape from the stove and rise to the ceiling.

'Stop!' Lena says, not stopping.

Bitten on her neck, her arm, her breast, Lena bleeds into the dish drainer. Her bra all bug-eyed in the sink. The single glass left winking there from the summer, splattered and lustrous with blood.

'Ouch,' she says, pulling away when her tongue is bitten. Feet have smeared the fallen droplets. Outside, the dog, Hamlet, bays. Let him in, for godsakes, Lena says. So very hot now in the cabin, brilliant brilliant heat. No dog needed. Not just yet.

Oh, polite and socially responsible owners of this place. Oh, neat and kempt girl from the mainland. Blood is life. Swarming with existence. Blood sausage. Blood pancakes on Fridays. Blood soup. Raw meat slurking through brown paper bags on the train, staining the laps of commuters. The dog, sniffing out something good, bellows at the door. Lena twists upon Soile's hand. Malaria lives in blood and worms swim in the rosy tubes and merry corkscrews twirl and dance, happy to bring their little surprises your way, and there is always always AIDS. Those needles in the dumpsters. She's not one to make the living suffer.

How fine and warm is Soile now. How beautiful. 'What are you?' she asks Lena again. She smiles. Her teeth. She bends down and puts her lips on the white forehead.

The hair is long, Swedish yellow-white, good hair to stuff your boots with. She cuts with scissors first, *schwick, schwick*, but then with knives, Lena now so silent. There was a cap, a knitted one, red wool and pompom, near the fishing poles. On it goes, to keep that little head warm while dinner is prepared. Such big eyes she has. Will you have some cake and wine with me, my darling? Some liver? Naked but for your sweet red cap. Come. Hold my hand now. I am warm with all this joy. You will love me soon.

The summer village empty. All the people gone to places other. Dreaming dreams of toast and cheese and granny nodding in her bed. This colour red, the winking glass, the dripping tongue not part of dreaming. The second step is always damp in summer. The foot pulls back from all that cold. By lunchtime, though, the wood is dry.

The Telephone of the Dead

Marnie Gottfried's husband, Steve, had been dead for two weeks when he called her for the first time. She had just returned from Israel, hadn't even unpacked, was as unhinged and raw as she would ever be, and the telephone call sent her windmilling to a therapist. When she mentioned the telephone call to the polite little man, he prescribed something, but even after she was regularly swallowing anti-hallucinogenic chemicals, the calls continued. In fact, she got a three-thousand–dollar telephone bill, collect charges from an 800 service distressingly called The Telephone of the Dead. She didn't share this with the therapist, surmising - quite correctly - that he would think she was hooked up with some necrophiliac outfit.

Her husband had come home in a summer storm, the clouds boiling like a pot of scummy soup, his little Citroën pulling between the pines as she bent to wring out the mop in the kitchen. The lightning was directly overhead, had - in fact - hit the chimney *again* and fried the computer. She was growing tired of changing the surge protector, bored with the childlike scream the computer made when struck by lightning. It simply wasn't true that lightning didn't strike the same place twice. It had favourite places, places like *their* chimney and *their* pines, where it loved to run riot, cavort wantonly, drive deeply into the earth again and again like a serial rapist.

It was sensible of Steve not to try to make it to the house

through an electrical storm. She peered out the kitchen window at the car, waved, but couldn't see a thing. The rain vomited down, uncontrollable, the thunderous belly noises deafening, truly. She finished mopping the floor, dumped the water down the drooling toilet and was heating up the meatloaf when Steven opened the back door.

'I think I've been hit by lightning,' he said, in an odd high voice strung through with glass. Freshets of water ran from his clothes onto her brilliantly waxed floor, and he held his arm out to her. On the soft, white part, just below the elbow, was a circle of red, covered with a bunch of soggy tissues. She reached out to brush them off but he screamed, 'Don't! It's my *skin*, Marnie!' The fur on his arm was gone except for a few shrivelled hairs that turned to ash as she watched.

'I told you not to go out in a storm,' she said. 'I warned you.'

He looked at her strangely, not at all with his usual obsequious good humour.

'I think I died,' he said, cradling his arm and rocking slowly forwards and back. He still stood, dripping on her floor. His hair noodled down his face and into his eyes.

'You're just being melodramatic,' she said. 'Put those clothes in the bathroom. You're ruining the floor. How did you really burn your arm? Starbucks?'

'No,' he said, 'something hit me. I fell flat on my back. I was looking up at the trees, the rain all but drowning me. I felt some part of me lift up out of my body, out of my eyes, but I could still see the house and Polly in her crib and you. You were waxing the floor.'

It gave her a jolt when he said that. He never noticed anything in the house. It wasn't even a good guess, because he had no clue that she ever cleaned the floors. He thought they stayed sanitary through sheer force of will. He thought shirts arrived from the Garden of Eden, freshly starched, and lined up in his closet, clinking and jostling to be first in line. He hadn't graduated from magical thinking.

'There was a bright light. I know this sounds like everyone else's story, people who almost die, but it really happened. I was pulled along towards the light and I could taste things in the air. Colours. I don't know. The further I went, the better I felt – light and free and warm, so warm. By God! It was fantastic! I didn't want to return, but I felt myself being dragged backwards. I bumped into my body and a squirrel was scrabbling onto me, trying to climb onto my face. Out of the wet.'

'Well!' she said. 'How's that for selfish? You'd have left me and Polly and Ronnie just to be warm and free? Nice! Where's your sense of responsibility?'

He looked at her with deep loathing. Something squirmed across his face and ran down into his collar.

'You're the selfish one,' he said, 'wanting me to give that up.'

He pushed past her, imprinting his wet clothes on her cotton sundress, went upstairs and slammed the door to their bedroom. He didn't unlock the door or come down again until he went out for tests the next morning. The doctors claimed he would be fine, except for possible blindness. That he would live to one hundred and tell his grandchildren the story of how he had been hit by lightning in his own backyard, but he still hadn't spoken to Marnie when he died of a heart attack three days later. Silly man.

'Darling,' he said, on a Friday afternoon, the first time he called and she knew it was him from the way his tongue skipped the r. It was a lucid dream, deliciously, comfortably real. Not worrisome at all. 'Have you paid the pool guy?'

'Why did you die?' she asked, floating pleasantly, bobbing in the late afternoon light, jetlagged and shell-shocked and tranquilised within an inch of her life.

'Heart attack,' he said, 'I thought you knew.'

'No, no. What I meant was ...' What *had* she meant? Why did you leave me? I *needed* you. I've been so angry that you wimped out of life, went AWOL. 'Are you all right? Is it nice there?'

'Oh, you're wondering about the three square meals, roof over your head kind of thing. It's not like that,' he said, 'but I'm feeling wonderful, better all the time.'

She didn't know what to say to that. She was feeling worse all the time. Every day dawning with a newer version of pain laid out for her to try on. Even though he hadn't been a fully satisfactory husband, she had been used to him, and relied on his company and help with the children. And, he'd had a regular pay cheque, was punctual with the bills.

'Where are you calling from? I didn't think ... I thought ... what kind of phone is it?'

'British,' he said immediately. 'Red phone booth. Smells like cigars and wood with a bad case of dry rot. Heavy, old-fashioned black receiver.'

And since she was dreaming, she *had* to be dreaming, she pictured Dr Who, beset by Daleks, purling through infinite space in a red telephone box. She was still laughing her new psychopathic laugh when he hung up on her.

The calls came often after that, always late on Friday afternoon, and there were many times when she was not in a drugged torpor, or dozing on the couch, or in a suggestible mood brought on by the death of one's thirty-seven year old husband, and the telephone bill made it quite impossible to suppress the belief that this wasn't some delusional coping method cooked up by her more officious neurons. It might be, it was, real.

He usually called her late in the afternoon, when she was on the couch, reading, Polly napping in her crib, Ronnie not yet home from school.

'So, how was your week?' he asked, as flat and disinterested as the asinine robot voice that had guided her through the flight arrival times in Israel. She wanted to say it had been hideous, horrible, the Grand Canyon of desperate weeks, but can you say that to a corpse?

'All right, I guess,' she said, 'Polly's cutting a tooth.'

She'd been dreaming away her days, but once night fell, her bedroom filled with cats in heat, chanting 'Now! Now! Nauwooo!' Their shrieking filled her ears; she was deaf to all but the lusting of invisible cats, and she certainly couldn't sleep. Polly had been hysterical when she finally went in to her, a glaze of snot over her entire face, shuddering and juddering and rigid with misery. 'What's the matter, Polly Wolly?' she'd asked, lifting the baby out of her crib. But her daughter had stared at her as if she had turned into a fluorescent midnight Medusa, and screamed piercingly, striking at Marnie's face and clawing at her eyes. In the morning, there was a sliver of ivory glowing in Polly's swollen gum, and a two-inch scratch on her own eyelid.

'Mmm,' he said and he may as well have said, 'Who's that?' His memory was cotton candy, fairy floss, things melting at the edges, and poor Polly must have been at the edge, a newborn memory with too few sticky strands spun around her.

'Your youngest child. A girl,' she said, prompting him. Steve had brought Polly to nurse at night. He'd massaged the infant with almond oil, tracing circles on her heels with his thumbs. He'd carried her everywhere, draped over one forearm, like a butler's towel. The room slid by sideways, the sun darting happy summertime spears into her eyes. Polly was the baby who had slept between them for three months and kept them apart. Close. Apart.

'So, how was your week?' he asked again and then, before she had a chance to answer, she heard him talking to someone else, a woman. 'Just a moment, Madam.' Was he talking to her? When had she become Madam? Her husband, Steve, was softly pleading with another woman, a kind of moan in his voice and, dear God, it made her heart race. Had the Arabs got it right and fifty virgins waited for a good man in Paradise? Was he, even as he spoke to her, being massaged, fondled by some unearthly nymphet?

'Steve?' she called, clutching the phone and willing her auditory centres to amplify those bleached sounds of climactic urgency.

'*Excuse me* ... I'm talking to my wife. Let go!'

She heard scuffling, rustling, a crescendo of sound and was picturing imminent ecstasy at the hands or mouth of someone remarkably like Shula, her husband's sexy assistant, the one she'd made him get rid of, when a smoker's voice, a voice plugged with gravel and clay, totally unfamiliar, came boiling down the line.

'Mommy!' it drawled, 'I ran away and was *killed*. You don't have to keep on putting my pictures on the milk cartons. You don't ...'

'I'm sorry,' she said, 'I'm not your mother. I have my own little children. I'm ...' and for a moment she couldn't remember her own name, and only the sound of her dead husband's voice, begging in the background – 'Marnie! Marnie! Let go, you harpy! Let me speak to my wife!' – was capable of reminding her. 'I'm Marnie Gottfried,' she said. 'From New Haven.'

'I want my mommy!' the thing wailed. 'How does this stupid phone work?' which was Marnie's own question. It might be like black holes, or the Bermuda Triangle, or conception. Subject to theories but difficult to prove.

'What's your name?' she asked the murdered thing, whose voice pelted her ears with gobbets of red clay and tiny bullets of granite. 'Can you remember your name?'

But the girl, the murdered one, bayed and there was a noise of beating leathery wings, and that awful wolflike howl, drawn out endlessly and magnified over the line, and once, in the middle of it, she heard Steve croak, 'Marnie?' and then a new voice said, 'Who is this? Are you God?' This was a streetwalker's voice, still chewing air gum, still with traces of mascara in it. Behind this voice, she could hear her husband remonstrating with the murdered girl and then there was screaming, a catfight in paradise, and things were said that made her hair rise, her tail, if she'd had one, would have been a liatris. When she could no longer hear her husband's voice, she lay the telephone back in its plastic bed and sat in her floral Queen Ann chair, as still as a corpse, until the room was utterly shrouded in darkness.

A week later, he was calling again.

'So,' he said, 'how was your week?'

'What the hell was that?' she asked, still bruised from the howling.

'What?' he said, and he sounded like Ronnie, caught stealing a freeze pop. Incredulous that you suspected him of wrongdoing.

'The harpy, the whore, I mean, who's in charge of room assignments?'

'The boss, of course.'

'Oh,' she said, nonplussed. 'That makes sense.' She could have kicked herself. Nothing made sense. Nothing. 'Why do you always call me on Friday afternoon?'

'That's when they let us out.'

And this truly silenced her. Out of where? She didn't like to think of the possibilities when she thought of the others who stood in line with him to use the telephone.

Ronnie ploughed through the summer, not looking right or left, no longer loving Mrs Brown, the camp director, no longer talking to his friends, ex-friends, because they couldn't understand the foreign language that came out of his mouth. His father had died. They knew that, secretly imagined what it would be like if their own fathers disappeared from the dinner table, and some of them – the divorced kids – thought they knew what it felt like, thought they felt the same wound running from the top of their heads to the seat of their spines, splitting them in half; the operation performed with a dull bread knife, the sawing, the hacking unceasing until they were divided. Yeah. They thought they knew. And as they passed him, some of them blurted the things their parents had told them to say: 'Sorry' and 'Too bad' and 'He was a nice man' and 'Where did the lightning hit him?' But mostly he was ignored and that was just fine. He wanted to finish circle time and pinch potting and banana boating, turn in his projects and get graded on what kind of kid lets his father get killed. He wanted – more than anything – to lie in the earth and stare up at the sky until he drifted up there too. Until his insides leaked out and evaporated, became clouds and rain and lake and ocean and clouds again.

This was all written on his face and his friends avoided him because of it, but when he came home, Marnie held his hands, hugged him, washed him with the rough washcloth, sat too close, touching, touching, not letting go.

'How was your day?' she asked. 'Anything special happen?'

Her words ran over him like water, meaningless. He slung his backpack in the closet and went to sit in the Citroën. She wanted him to see a kiddie psychiatrist, a Virginia Axline, a sandtray therapist, where he could bury little coffins and drive little Citroëns round and round plastic pine trees and torpedo his mother with Playmobil bombs right where she stood mopping the floor.

The gym teacher from camp called – a morning call, a call she picked up callously, knowing it wasn't Steve – and asked if there was a history of seizures in the family.

'I'm talking petit mal here,' he said. 'Eyelids fluttering, spacing out momentarily. Sound familiar?'

'Why?' she said, scanning the outrageous bill from the telephone company, a bill she'd have to argue: Israeli hotel, Middle Eastern long-distance calls, the Telephone of the Dead.

'... Ronnie on the floor.'

She'd missed what he was saying. 'That's fine,' she said. 'He's fine. We're all fine. Thanks for your concern.'

And she'd hung up thinking they *were* fine. They were alive. It was Steve who had the problem.

In her garden, the next morning, with pads like monstrous mushroom caps strapped to her knees, she sunk her hands as deeply as she could into the rotting soil. A thin root ran past her fingers, like an underground power cable, and when she blindly touched it, she received the smallest shock. It was a dandelion spearing down, obsessive in its desire to take over the earth. She encircled it, tightened her grip and yanked hard on it, downwards. The weed listed beneath the earth and she crowed. That was what it was like to be a mole or a gopher or a vole. Powerful. Subversive.

The phone began ringing, a ringing that struck her like an atomic blast, the windows of her home blowing out in fountains of glittering, somersaulting glass, but when it stopped, when she stood up to remove the fungal extrusions from her knees, the house was standing, the windows staring placidly at the sky.

Her husband's Citroën was still parked underneath the pines, and she began to wonder where she'd left the key. It would be like her, to have buried him with the key in his pocket, but she couldn't really remember. Shrouds probably didn't have pockets and the Chevra Kadisha had been adamant about protocol. No suits, no glasses, no notes from Ronnie, no teddy bear from Polly, no kisses, no flowers, no music, no mirrors.

She had found a letter in the top drawer of his desk, marked: 'To Be Opened in the Event of My Death' and, at first, it seemed like it had been written by another man. No mention was made of her or the children, or their rented house under the trees, or his job with the Whiffle Poofs, or any of it, and she thought the letter might have been written many years ago, before they'd had children, and he had forgotten to tell her about it. But the paper was the heavyweight Crane stuff she had bought him for their anniversary and the letter was dated the day before he'd died.

He had asked to be buried in the traditional way, the *religious* way, with the assistance of the Sacred Society, and he wanted to be buried in Israel. He had bought a plot for himself and an officious little yid showed up with the paperwork. She thought the man probably lived in the freezer down at the morgue, but it turned out he'd recently spoken to Steve on the phone and taken his credit card number and was only doing his job, delivering the deed. 'Such a young man. How sad,' he said as he handed her the manila envelope. Karka in Israel, which sounded like shit in Israel, but meant land in Israel. A tiny plot indeed, in the stony heart of the world. There was a slip with telephone numbers, names, the El Al flight schedule for God's sake. Steve had it all organised.

They'd never been religious people. Or, at least, she hadn't. She was no longer sure about Steve. Certainly they'd gone to a cocktail party on Yom Kippur the previous year, eaten treif in dozens of places. And now he wanted to be buried in Israel?

But she'd done it all. Followed his plans to the letter. Shlepped the casket to Israel on the plane, snuck in at night to polish the simple wooden box with lemon oil, only to see the anachronistic shtetl Jews in their black polyester shtetl suits pry off the lid, lift out Steve and lower his linen-swathed body into the crater. She had really cried then, seeing the Jerusalem rock pitched down onto his unprotected head, the ants already on the march, men from *Invasion of the Body Snatchers* rattling on in Hebrew. A heavily bearded woman had approached her, then muscularly ripped the collar off her best suit.

So the keys probably weren't in Steve's pocket.

In one of his first calls, she'd asked him why he wanted the religious funeral, but he hadn't answered. It mattered to her, though. She wanted to know.

'Steve,' she said, 'I had to go to *Israel*. My God! It's a Third World country. Always blowing themselves up. Polly and

Ronnie stayed with Mom. What were you thinking?'

'Thank you,' he said, 'it's a relief.'

'What is?' she said, almost screaming, almost scratching her eyes out.

'Being in the earth,' he said, and she heard the dull clunk of the rock hitting his skull. 'It's freeing.'

'Oh, freedom,' she said, 'that's all you care about. You don't care two hoots for your family. It's all about you. That lightning blew your fuses.'

'No. That's not it. The less there is of me *there* ...' he said, slowly, thinking it out as he said it, her throat closing as she realised he was using 'there' for the world, her world, her life, '... the more there is of me here.'

And where was *here*, exactly, besides a British telephone booth that was definitely somebody's idea of a funny joke?

'The worms and the beetles and the ants, they're important, they nibble through what connects the soul to the body. Like being tickled. Like picking off a scab. It feels good.'

She walked into Polly's room and stared at her daughter, wetly sucking her thumb in a real heaven. She held onto the edge of the crib and waved the telephone at the unhappy crawling things which swarmed from the walls. A different time, on a day when she felt stronger, she asked him about cremation, the designer label of being less in this world, and he choked. Gagged on her words.

'Don't!' he said, 'It's murder,' and he abruptly hung up.

He was a weak man, the kind to kowtow to *anyone*, bow down and lick the boots of the oppressor, just for personal advancement, just to get ahead, and it revolted her. When they'd first come to New Haven, before they had children, he'd taken her downtown to see the Yale campus. It was a summer evening, and as they walked along, peering into the frivolous shops and admiring the very Englishness of it all, she'd felt she might be able to love him. She could force it out of herself, like a bowel movement.

Her mother's succession of flaccid husbands appalled her, convinced her that Steve wasn't so bad. That he *must* be lovable, if only for the way his hair became transparent when it was wet, a quirk that had entirely charmed her when they were dating. But then, they'd turned down an arcade, and a man – a security guard, they thought – ran up behind them and pushed them along, his hands on the smalls of their backs. 'Sorry folks,' he said, 'I'm real sorry about this.' He made them sit on steps at the blind end of the arcade and they saw he was holding a long serrated knife and his eyes glowed and spun like marbles, and he shook from head to toe with something they couldn't identify. This man, this criminal, was wearing a bright Hawaiian shirt and red high-tops. 'I'd hate to cut you,' he said, as if he meant it, and she stood up then, behind her husband, ready to run or kick or bite or whatever was necessary to survive. Her husband's knees, she saw, were bludgeoning each other, his skin the colour of canvas.

'I need a fix, man, they're killing me here. They shut down all the hospitals, no one gives me a chance.'

They had seven hundred dollars in cash to pay the movers and it was a fortune to them then, but what the hell. Give the guy the money, she almost shouted. Almost kicked Steve in the back to get him moving. She wanted to get home in one piece, all her limbs attached. Steve took out his wallet and glanced inside at the thick bundle of twenties.

'I've got a twenty,' he mewled, 'but I need a ten for the

babysitter. Will you take a ten?'

The man sighed and lowered his knife. 'Damn it,' he said, 'I always get the Jews.'

He took the ten and walked quickly away, and her husband, the man who had been playing with their lives, turned and vomited on her shoes.

'You know,' he said, the next time he called, a humid afternoon full of greenflies and the shouts of children out of camp, 'if you'd do something for me, I wouldn't be stuck here with little Lolita and a bunch of anal anaesthesiologists. Flotsam.'

She was probably flotsam. Or maybe it was jetsam. She could never tell which was which. Or maybe she was ballast. The heavy bottom of things.

'Pardon?' she said. 'I thought you're beyond help at this point.'

She laughed, the mirth of the anchor chain as it is borne down into the depths of the sea.

'Not at all. The scuttlebutt around here is that you can get pretty decent accommodations if you suck up to the boss. Shmear him a little. What say you light the Shabbos candles. For me.'

Her mind boggled at the thought of shmearing God. Slipping Him a little bribe on the side. This really had to be a prank devised by some evil bastard down at the Whiffle Poofs. Or maybe it was those Skull and Bones boys.

'Marnie,' he said, 'are you still there?'

'What?' she said. Religious coercion direct from heaven or hell or wherever it is that dead people hang out. It was unbelievable. Despite his sadly depleted state, he was still forging ahead with his pathetic plans for advancement.

On hot summer days, driving home from work, Steve used to wind up the windows and turn on the ancient heating system in the Citroën. He wore three sweaters and two scarves, a woollen balaclava and a pair of rubber gardening gloves and, by the time he got home, his skin would be a bright, slippery purple, like the underside of a tongue. They had a claw-footed tub in the cellar, with a hose from outside hanging through the jalousie, cold water only. After parking the car under the pines, he'd come tearing through the house, and launch himself into the tub. There'd be screams from downstairs as the water hit his skin, and eventually yodelling. 'Great sauna,' was what he always said to her when he came upstairs wrapped in a towel. 'It's incredibly healthy for you. You should try it some day.'

At the yoga class he'd given her for her birthday, when she was supposed to be emptying her mind of distracting thoughts, she secretly pictured what would happen to him if he was stopped by the police dressed in his woollies and his gardening gloves, the heater blazing. She'd willed it to happen, pictured it so solidly that it seemed inevitable that he'd be pulled over and wind up in jail for at least a night. Get the breathalyser test. A cavity search. And the police officers would look at her with pity when she came to bail him out in the morning, and hand her the rubber gloves.

'How did you call me?' she asked Steve for what felt like the hundredth time. 'What is it that you say to the operator?'

She rubbed her thighs, warmed her hands in her armpits. Lately, she could never get warm. Some vital internal engine had turned off. She pinned the phone to her ear with her shoulder and blew on her hands.

'I already told you,' he said, 'I ask the operator to put me through to my wife. That's all. Listen. Are you going to light the candles? It has to be before sunset. None of that after-dark malarkey.'

'Who is Ronnie?' she asked. 'Who is Polly?' She paused, blew a single smoky breath into the ice-cold air. 'Who is Marnie?'

There was a silence at the other end, and the wind strummed the invisible telephone lines, plucking a deep B-flat that sung through the phone and susurrated through the marrow of her collarbone.

'My wife?' he guessed, his brain gone porous, licked down to the stick, freeing itself a little more each day.

'Oh, Steve,' she said. 'Yes. Your wife. And your children.' It was like being married to a victim of Alzheimer's who was locked up in some prestigious Long Island facility, making furtive phone calls when the staff wasn't looking. Not much of a marriage.

'You'll do it?' he asked, still puffing around his version of the fast track.

'I don't know. Maybe,' she said. 'Listen, Steve. I'm just not into all that claptrap.'

He began to give her the telephone number of the local Chabad House, where she could pick up a brochure of candle lighting times, and she felt her fingers tightening into talons around the receiver.

'No!' she shouted, louder than she'd intended. 'Forget it. I'm not doing it.'

There was a hiccup and then, loud and clear down the line, the sound of Steve crying. 'You don't really love me. You never loved me. If you did, you'd light the damned candles and get me out of this armpit.'

It reminded her of when he begged for oral sex. 'If you really loved me,' he'd whined, 'you'd swallow.' But he'd cried then too.

It was the usual way he gave her a guilt trip, to get her to do what he wanted.

'Oh, stop it,' she said. 'I'll think about it.'

It was ghastly: a shade, a spirit, a dybbuk telling her what to do, but offering nothing in return. So utterly selfish. It shocked her (although after the telephone booth nothing would ever truly shock her in all her long life) that the World-to-Come could be so base, so *craven*. And what was the deal with the telephone? A backdoor business line? They call out for pizza when the staff goes on strike? They call the riot police when the harpy goes canine?

She'd received calls now from Steve at Ronnie's camp and once at the gym and once when she was visiting her mother in Boston, so she knew that the simple request, 'Put me through to my wife' would connect them, wherever she was. Or he was. It was maddening. She'd never wanted a cell phone, that degree of connectedness feeling like an invasion. And yet, here was her husband, ex-husband, whatever, trailing her through the woods of her life like a bloodhound.

One particularly hot Friday afternoon, as she lay on the couch, idling, there was a miserable thunk, the lights went out and the air conditioner stopped working. She went down to the basement to reset the circuit-breaker and it was there, in the darkness, that she knew what was amiss. The power had been cut off. An image of the last five cheques she'd written swam in front of her eyes, cheques she didn't have the money to cover. Sweat crept down her back like an insect. Unless she got a job, she and Polly and Ronnie would soon be on a cat-food diet. 'Ronnie?' she called, climbing the stairs. 'Polly? Who wants to go to Grandma's?' She found Polly asleep in her crib, splayed out like a starfish, but Ron didn't answer. 'Ron? Ronnie?' she called as she walked through the house, horribly aware that she had no idea where Ronnie had been for the past six hours. Since breakfast, in fact. Some mother.

She searched through the garden and the mildewed apple trees along the back fence. This is what desperation feels like, she thought. *Mounting desperation.* She glanced at the Citroën, still parked under the pine trees after its last unlucky trip. The windows were fogged up, a lopsided heart and 'Daddy' scrawled across the windshield. Ronnie was in the car, slumped on the driver's seat, wearing his father's sauna clothes: the thick woollen sweaters, the scarves, the balaclava, even the gardening gloves. He looked like a potato she'd once exploded in the microwave, his mouth open and foam on his lips. 'Ronnie,' she said, gently shaking his arm. 'Wake up.'

The car was incredibly hot and moist. She pulled his arm harder and when he still didn't move, slapped him on the backside. 'Get going, Ronnie. I've wasted enough time looking for you already. I'm not going to stand here all day.'

A humid breath stirred the pines and raised the hair on the back of her neck. 'Ronnie?' she said again. The little boy had the keys to the Citroën in his hand, and she pulled them away from him, taking in the slow slide of his rubbery arm to the floor of the Citroën before moaning, 'Oh God, no.' She shoved him over to the passenger seat and got in, started the car and revved the engine. 'Not Ronnie. God *damn* you Steve.' At every red light, she leaned over and squeezed the little foot that had somehow gotten hooked up on the ashtray. He was breathing. 'I'll get you there honey. You're going to make it.'

It was only when the policewoman was asking her yet again

how Ronnie had come to be parboiled in a car, how he hadn't been noticed for *so many hours*, and why it was, exactly, that he was wearing all those heavy clothes, that she remembered another important thing she had forgotten: Polly, at home in her crib. 'Excuse me,' she said to the policewoman, who eyed her as if she was something that fell out of a vacuum cleaner bag. 'I'm just going to dash home and pick up some pyjamas.' When the woman made a move as if to stop her, she added, 'For Ronnie.' The woman nodded, but said, 'If you're not back in twenty minutes, I'll have to issue a warrant for your arrest.'

'Do you think it was deliberate?' Marnie wailed. 'That I'm an abusive mother?' The policewoman stared at her and said nothing. Dear God, what would happen if she found out about Polly?

The phone was ringing as she pulled up under the pines, and she ran to answer it, afraid it was bad news about Ronnie, but it was only Steve.

'So,' he said. 'How was your week?'

'You bastard!' she screamed. 'You couldn't call and tell me about Ronnie?'

'Ronnie?' he said, and she let the last good memory of her husband go, felt it slide out of her like his semen.

'Your son. Look. I'm too busy to talk right now. I've got to get back to the hospital.'

There wasn't a sound from Polly's room. She had a premonition that the baby had died in her crib. She pictured the little girl strangled in the Mickey Mouse bumpers; smothered, face down, in her own vomit; her head caught between the bars of the crib. The silence chattered demonically at her nerves. But Polly was still sleeping, thumb in her mouth, a ring of mustard yellow baby poo on the leg of her onesie. It was oddly annoying to find her alive.

'I'm just checking,' Steve said. 'You have the candles, right?'

'I don't want you to call me any more. I want you to stop this. It's abusive, it's ... just leave me alone. Okay, Steve? Please. You have no idea what I'm going through.'

'Did you speak to the rabbi yet?'

'Steve. Stop. Your son, Ronnie, is in the hospital right now. He's badly dehydrated, unconscious. I really have to go.'

The house smelled like rotting flowers, like pseudomonas. The flowers that people had sent after she returned from Israel were still on every surface in their cheap florists' vases. Dead. That was the stink. The flowers were all dead.

'You're not going to drive to the hospital on the Sabbath are you?'

She came close then to using a word she had avoided her entire life. She could taste it on her tongue like a lozenge of wasabi, bringing the water to her eyes.

The next morning, she woke, blinking against the staleness of Ronnie's hospital room and the fug of Polly's breath on her face, hearing Steve's voice whispering over and over, like a dog snuffling at her heels, 'Put me through to my wife. Put me through to my *wife*.' Her brain stalled but then started with a roar. He was only able to connect with her by asking for his wife. She watched several cute young doctors and a gentle-faced middle-aged man walk by. Suddenly, they all looked like possibilities. Ways to get away from Steve. She inquired of a passing nurse if there was internet access available for the patients, left Polly in the reclining chair they'd slept in and trotted down the hall in her fluffy slippers. In the patients' lounge, she turned on one of the computers. The screen flickered, green letters sprinting across the abyss. She swivelled her chair to face the screen, typed in *online dating services*, and pressed Search.

Marnie read every one of the Happy Endings, peering at the faces of the men to see if they looked as if they might have a job with the Whiffle Poofs. If they might have been barbecued under some pine trees on a hot summer day. None of them did. They looked cool and scrubbed, like new cars in a dealership, still smelling faintly of plastic.

The Lady and the Leper

She was a quiet woman. She had been a quiet woman all her days, a silent observer of those around her. Her face like the smooth surface of a pond, her movements uncoordinated, her manner of dress chosen to be inconspicuous, her nails bitten, a quartet of round scars on the back of her right hand.

She liked to walk in the woods whether they were full of snow or mud or golden light or the decaying smell of fallen leaves. She liked to lie on the fecund ground and cover herself with twigs and moss and let the small life of the place crawl across her skin. She liked to call to the birds from deep within her mind and imagine that they called back to her. She liked to stare at clouds until they evaporated. Her family thought she was very strange. The neighbours whispered the C-word and tapped their foreheads.

She never noticed.

'Hello bird!' she called out as she walked. 'Hello cow! Hello beetle! Hello lichen!'

One day, in her forty-sixth year, she saw a man walking in her woods, and she hid behind a burr oak until she thought he had left. But when she stepped out, the man still stood there, staring solemnly at her.

She raised her hand, almost as if she might wave, but then put the traitor behind her back. 'Hello, man,' she said.

'Hello, lady,' said the man. His voice sounded like the oak

tree. His eyes looked like the sky. She flinched and covered her face with her hands.

'Goodbye,' she said, and walked away.

It was late autumn. When she had gone far enough, she sat and drew a blanket of fallen leaves over her body and lay back to soak her eyes in the sky. A sharp-shinned hawk flew overhead and, a few seconds later, his shadow touched her face. She could still hear Man walking away, down the path to the main road.

'Hello bird!' It was not her voice. She put her fingers on her lips to check. She had not said that. It was him. 'Hello squirrel!' His voice, calling greetings to the forest, grew fainter. Very softly, she said again, 'Goodbye Man.' A leaf spiralled through the slanting light and patted her cheek. She sat up and pulled the petiole through the top buttonhole of her indifferent blouse.

There were no leaves on the trees the next time Man came to the forest. His footprints left pale blue depressions in the skin of the snow, his voice called to the mink and the deer and the wild turkey.

'Hello Lady,' he said, when he saw her.

She clutched her elbows and looked away.

'Hello Lady,' he said again.

'Hello Man,' she said, very low.

'Did you see the turkey?' he asked, as if he expected an answer.

She shook her head. She glanced at his face. He was looking at her. She took a step backwards and tripped.

'You fell,' he said, not looking at her anymore.

'Yes,' she said, pulling snow over her scarred legs.

'That will be cold.' It was said without judgement.

She wanted to say that under the snow it was warm, but she

noticed that it was, indeed, cold. Her voice did not work.

He sat down in the snow some distance from her. 'I am a leper,' he said, his hands twittering in his lap.

'Oh,' said Lady. She glanced at him. She had not expected him to sit near her. She had not expected him to speak. 'What is that?'

'You don't know?' said Man. He began to explain it to her. 'I am not like other men. See these marks on my skin? I carry within me a kind of poison. I cannot live with people from your world because I am contagious. I can only live with other men who are also lepers.'

'That's all right,' she said. 'I don't mind.' She looked at him. 'I'm a bit like that myself.' He looked at her. They did not look away from each other.

'My sickness used to ride with cancer or pneumonia. Now it rides with leprosy.'

A tear stood like a raindrop in the sky of Man's eye. Lady was not frightened of what he had told her. She was frightened because of the tear.

'Goodbye Man,' she said, and she stood and stumbled between the trees and was gone.

Man walked to where she had been sitting. The snow had melted under her body. He took an acorn out of his pocket and lay it in one of her handprints. The wind blew his red scarf against his face, and on it, he could smell the sweet odour of the sheep whose hair had made the scarf, and the silver smell of the snow, and his own Man smell. He loved the smell of Man.

'Goodbye Lady,' he said, and he turned to walk down the hill.

Later that winter, they met again on the highest path, where the incessant wind had blown the snow from the rocky tors and twisted the trees into old men bent over with scoliosis.

'Hello Man,' said Lady. She took a step towards him. Her face was bright with the cold.

'Stop,' he said, holding up his hand. He was thinner, much thinner than he had been. 'Do not touch me. Remember. I am a leper.'

'Yes.' She shrank back. 'I'm sorry.'

'I'm sorry too,' he said, and he took a step towards her in apology.

'Stop,' she said, and this time it was her who held up her hand. 'I am afraid.' And this time, it was he who shrank back.

They looked at each other. They were both ashamed.

'Your eyes are blue,' she said. 'Like the sky.'

'The ends of your hair are red,' he said.

'Are they?' said Lady. She touched her hair. She did not know what colour her hair was, but Man said the ends were red.

They stood in silence. The wind blew and blew. His scarf and her hair, snapping against their skin, like whips.

'There were little footprints from the sparrows on my doorstep this morning,' she said eventually. 'They looked like arrows.'

'Beautiful!' he said, and she smiled, and then he smiled, and then they both blinked and shrank back.

'Goodbye,' they said at the same moment. Trembling. It was very cold.

'Oh!' said Lady. 'Wait. Please. I have something. For you.'

'Don't give me anything,' he said. 'You mustn't give me things.' He fed his hands to his pockets and leaned away from her. The cutting wind had put tears in his eyes.

She pulled a red knitted hat from inside her coat and laid it in on the ground.

'It's not much and it's not very good anyway. You could just leave it there. It didn't take long to make,' she said and her voice was as high as a bird's and she let the wind carry her away before she spoke the last word. 'Goodbye.'

Just before the trees, she turned and lifted her hand. He watched until she was out of sight and then bent and picked up the hat. It was soft and still warm. It smelled of her. He did not like her smell, of lichen and forest duff and bark. He liked his own Man smell. He put the hat in his back pocket to make it his and not hers anymore.

From within the trees, Lady saw him pick up the hat, and she put a hand to her mouth. But then he put the hat in his pocket and walked away bareheaded. 'Oh,' she said. 'Oh.' He did not want her gift.

She still loved the forest. She still loved the sky. She still called out greetings to the salamanders and skinks. She still let the moist brown earth leave its fingerprints on her skin. But now she also listened for the footfalls of Man, his Man sounds, and knew she missed something when he did not come. And now, she pressed her fingertips into the round scars on the back of her hand, to remind herself not to listen for him, to remind herself that men were dangerous, and the wind blew tiny waves across the pond of her face. She wished for the stillness before Man. The peace.

'What do you wish for?' she asked him, the next time they met.

'A companion,' he said. 'A leper, like me. What do you wish for?'

But she did not know what she wished for. Each finger on her left hand pressed against a scar on the back of her right hand. She pressed so hard that there were bruises afterwards.

'I am not a leper,' she said.

'No,' he said kindly, looking into her eyes. 'You are not.'

She could see it on him, that he was a leper, and she saw that he was dying slowly, but she was not afraid. He believed her also, that she was timid. Sometimes it seemed to her that this believing each other was very profound. Sometimes she thought it was merely what ordinary people did everyday. She knew she was not like other people. She thought Man was closer to being like ordinary people than she was.

In early spring, she saw him walking slowly up the path from the main road and he was wearing the hat she had knitted, even though it did not fit well. She thought his head would stay warm now, and then felt her face grow hot with pleasure and something else she could not name. That hot feeling in her skin frightened her and, though Man searched for her, she hid from him and wept into the bole of the scarlet oak.

'I have brought you something too,' he called, and when she peeked, she saw that he held a small box in his hands and he turned painfully in a circle so that she might see it from wherever she was hiding. He knew she was hiding.

He pinched a tiny brass key on the side of the box between his fingers and twisted it several times and then opened the lid. A soft and tinkly sound came out and a spray of chickadees rose into the air, chipping and wheeling. Lady had never seen a music box. She had never heard music. To her, the simple tune was as beautiful as that of a house finch, a waterfall of liquid song that cracked open a tiny glass vial she had not known was hidden in the centre of her chest.

'Oh!' she said, and put her hand on her heart to feel the shards of glass. To catch what the vial had contained.

'Lady?' called Man again. 'This is a music box. It plays "Greensleeves" when you turn this key. I've wanted to give it to you for a while. I thought you might like it.' And he lay the pretty thing down on a piece of bark and turned away.

'Goodbye Man,' whispered Lady. She was vibrating as if the cold wind of winter still blew. She thought she was ill. Very ill. As ill as him.

He didn't return for a long time then, and Lady walked in the woods alone, the music box in her hand. There was a painting of a violet on the lid, and she had touched the picture so often that it had begun to fade, just like the spring violets themselves. When she turned the key and the box sang, she could no longer hear the sounds of the forest. The shy birds flew away ahead of her. The deer bounded off down the hills, their pert white tails raised in alarm. The forest was empty.

Late in spring, though, Man returned, and he brought with him a pair of binoculars, the better to see the birds in their nests, and a cough that shook his frame. He thought Lady might like to see the white ring around the eye of the robin, the transparency of the feet of the finch, and he had smiled to himself at the thought of her pleasure in these things.

She met him near the road, in a place where he had never seen her before. He thought she might have been waiting for him in the way that women sometimes wait for men, but then put the idea from his mind. She knew, after all, that he was a leper. She knew his love of Man.

'Man!' she said, and smiled, before covering her smile with her hand.

'Hello, my Lady,' he said, low and solemn. He, too, smiled at her. 'Look. I have brought binoculars.'

She put her head on one side. She did not know what binoculars were, but did not like to say so.

'Oh,' she said, and looked at the ground, where a wood louse lay curled in a ball.

'Come on,' said Man, beckoning. 'And you will see something interesting.'

She swallowed down her fear and walked after him, her eyes on the leather strap around his neck as if it were a snake hanging there, or an explosive. The back of his neck ran smoothly up onto his head and the skin was fine and rose-coloured, despite the lesions, and the muscles slid beneath the surface in a way she found disturbing. He was a beautiful animal.

This thought caused her face to burn and her feet to slow, but he adjusted his pace to hers and looked back often to make sure she was with him, and this too, caused her to walk slower and slower till eventually she stopped and put down roots, and then he turned and said, 'What is wrong, Lady?'

She raised her eyes to look into his but he could not read her thoughts, though they were writ there plain.

'Are you tired?'

She nodded her head once, abject, and looked away from him, towards the forest and the great swaying mass of leaves.

'There,' she said, pointing, 'an ivory-billed woodpecker.'

Man put the binoculars to his eyes.

'Hello woodpecker,' he said and then held out the glasses to her. They swung on their strap, one swing, two swings. A mockingbird called.

'Go on,' he said, leaning closer. 'Take them.'

She took the binoculars awkwardly and, to please him, pressed the glasses against her eyes. Tears blinded her.

'Do you see him?' asked Man, and then he saw that she was not even looking in the right direction. 'Lady,' he said, but then he said nothing more.

'I can see a tree,' she said in defence, but it was not true. She could see nothing and was ashamed of it.

'Lady,' said Man again, and he stood closer yet and his voice was as quiet as an earthworm under leaves. He did not want to frighten her. 'Look at what you want to see, and then lift the binoculars up to your eyes.' He turned away so she could try it without being witnessed.

'Hello woodpecker,' she said.

'Yes,' he said.

'Hello ash. Hello morel.' She turned the glasses on him. 'Hello Man.'

'Hello Lady,' he said, and took back the binoculars, blushing.

When his hand closed on the strap, her hand was still there, and for a moment, they touched.

'Oh!' she said. 'Now I will be like you.'

He had seen the four burns on the back of her hand and knew them for what they were.

'No you won't,' he said, but she was already gone.

Lady stood still in the forest. She stared up at a pale blue rectangle of sky and a sound came from her throat. It was the song of the music box. She had buried the music box under the oak where she had first seen Man. One day, twisting the key, she had heard a ping and a whirr and after that, the box no longer sang. It had died. Now the song rose from her throat. Slow and rusty. Unsure. The birds quieted in their branches and listened. And the wind that moved through that ancient precinct sighed.

She met Man several more times that spring and grew accustomed to his binoculars and the scent of him in the forest and his nearness. She waited for him openly at the beginning of the path, and he knew she had somehow gone beyond believing him, and he did not know how to remind her without hurting her, and so the days and weeks went by, and the fledglings learned to fly and gathered in trees distant from their nests and the butterflies emerged and pumped their bedraggled wings and mated high in the sky and laid their eggs on the milkweed pods at the edge of the boggy places and died, and the apples ripened on the wild apple tree.

On one of those late summer days, when they met, Lady said the apples were sweet, and he, not knowing of the apple tree, followed her to the clearing and the hairy old tree at the heart of the forest.

'Hello tree,' she said and curtseyed.

'Hello apples,' he said, saluting.

They stood together in the long grass, part of the symphony of cicadas and crickets and hot golden sunlight.

'No binoculars today,' she said.

'No.'

'The apples are good. Will you taste one?'

She set off and then turned to look back at him.

'Are you coming?'

He pulled his fingertips down the deep grooves that ran from the side of his nose to his lips. His skin now was transparent and falling.

'Lady,' he said.

'What?' she replied, frowning. The sun was in her eyes. She could not see his face. She could not see *him*.

'I am a leper.'

'Yes,' she said. 'I know.' But it seemed to him that she did not know. That she no longer wanted to know him in the way he truly was.

He trailed after her and, when they both stood under the embrace of the tree, he said again, very softly, 'I am a leper. I love Men. Do you understand, Lady?'

She did not respond. She twisted an apple and lifted its weight in her hand to pluck it from the branch, but as she stepped back to give it to him, there was a hiss and a snake moved under her foot and, startled, she fell. It was only a garter snake. Nothing dangerous.

'Hello snake,' she said, bending the grasses to cover the long burn scars on her legs. 'Look Man. There is a snake come to see us.'

Man knelt in the grass next to her. As he bent forward, Lady raised her hand and pressed her palm into the diseased skin that hung from his cheekbone. He turned and looked at her.

'No, Lady,' he said. His voice was louder than usual. 'You cannot touch me. I am a leper.'

'But I want to. This is what I wish for,' said Lady. 'I wish to be like you.' Her head was down upon her chest. He could barely hear her when she said, 'For then you would love me.' The apple lay forgotten in the grass. She licked her palm and rubbed it across the open wound on the back of her right hand. Her back curled over. Slowly, slowly, she became smaller and smaller, pulling into herself until she was a tiny thing upon the ground, as small and round as the apple.

The Seventeen Reasons I Hate You

Lennie put down *Suicide for Dummies* and leaned back. His house was clean. His bed was made. He'd just seen his regular hooker and had his hair cut. He'd killed all the bugs and said goodbye to all the women he'd caught staring at his ass. There was nothing, *nothing* left to do.

He lived in Florida's Century Village with ten thousand other old folks, smuggling in their cats and their budgies, their weed, their grandchildren (no poop in the pool!), their illicit pay from the Bagel Nook, the Lettuce Entertain You and the Phuket Thai; all trying to forget whatever their lives had been *before* and adjust to what it looked like now. The emptiness. The crappy little golf carts whirring between the cement condos with absurd English names like Derbyshire. For example. And of course he'd been given the D condo. Derbyshire D. It should have been F.

Bits of his former life rubbed shoulders with his now: the beer sign from his New Jersey bar blinked behind a huge sofa he'd picked up at the Goodwill; the signed photo of John Gotti hung over his bed, shutting up the pest control men who came for the roaches. There was a picture on the fridge of his daughter with her cat, taken about a week before she died. The daughter. Not the cat. The cat had hung on, frazzled and randy and vicious, until he'd beaten it to death with a straw broom. He'd been sweeping, goddammit, and the ugly survivor had snatched at the straw and almost knocked him off his pegs. That's the kind of animal it was. Didn't even have the guts to melt quietly in the dumpster, but rotted and stunk and all the neighbours complained and he'd had to go back there, still red-eyed from his daughter's shiva, and the bloody thing was moving from all the maggot action as if it was still alive.

After that, there'd been a time when he got up, walked outside in boxers that had lost their elastic and fell asleep in the sun until it was dark again, and then sat up all night, unable to breathe.

A woman walking her (illegal) dog. The cough when it pulls against its leash. The baby breeze creeping up his back and touching the sexy place behind his ears. Invisible birds making dumbass bird sounds. The small bits of stuff floating in the air that he used to think were fairies. A couple walk past, talking. He can't see their faces. He doesn't care. They lean towards each other. Chuckle. Such a soft sound. One of them, the woman, is a thalidomide kid, the kind with tiny amorphous arms. She waves her flipper in his direction. 'Good morning Lennie! How are you feeling?' Freakshow. Why did they save her sorry life? She makes his skin crawl. He closes his eyes. Orthopaedic shoes make a sound just like a horse walking in sawdust at the racetrack. The sun rises above the trees and smacks him directly in the forehead, making him forget. Light like a mortician. If he opens his eyes, he sees only darkness for a while.

It was during one of these naps that he first met Rosie. 'Yoo hoo,' she said. 'Can you help me over here?' She was spraying the plastic flowers outside her condo with perfume she'd shoplifted from the pharmacy. She sprayed him too. Now he checks on her each morning before leaving for work. She's ninety-four and lives right next door to him. He'd never seen her before. She wasn't an early riser.

Each morning, when he goes in to her condo, she's lying on her recliner in a see-through baby-doll outfit, the TV on snow.

'Rosie, darlin',' he says. 'Time to wake up, honey.'

She puckers up her lips. 'Give us a kiss then, dollface.'

Which he does, chastely, on the lips, before laying a blanket over all that forlorn flesh and asking if she needs anything at the drugstore or has any doctors' appointments. She makes the appointments after he knocks off from work so he can drive her and make sure the doctors don't get frisky and hopefully take her out to dinner afterwards, an early bird special at the Orchid Gardens.

A week ago, he found her lying on the floor, the back of the old recliner unhinged.

'Rosie!' he'd shouted. 'Oh God! Rosie! Are you okay?'

She cracked open one eye and puckered up her lips. 'Give us a kiss and I'll tell you, eh, sugarbutt?' Her eyelids were not attached to her eyeballs anymore, and the lower ones fell open and drooped wetly on her cheeks. Inside, the skin was an improbable bright orange. 'Tattooed,' she'd said when he asked her about it. 'Like my eyebrows.'

He kissed her and lifted her twiggy nest of a body onto the couch. 'I'm fine,' she said. 'I'll run the vacuum at your place after lunch, sexpot. And no. I don't need a thing today.' Already, he imagined a black something blooming on her back.

Later, predictably, she'd called him at work and said she'd bought a new recliner over the phone, at Target, and could he go get it for her. She needed it right away, she said, because the couch had begun to talk to her and it had a Polish accent and it was complaining about her bra size, and did he know there'd been a used condom under his bed when she vacuumed? She giggled and said that a tissue had been adequate back in the day, but she applauded his attention to cleanliness. She still thought his usual hooker was the exterminator.

He assumed it was the Target near Century Village, over to Federal Highway. It had shaken him up, seeing Rosie collapsed on her back like Joe Frazier. Stupid recliner. Probably made in Taiwan to break in a couple of months, so you'd be forced to buy another one and yet another one. He rolled his shoulders. He'd like to kill the fuckwits that made such defective merchandise.

'No need to curse,' said the store assistant. 'We have nothing here for a Rosie Moscowitz.' Lennie's gut growled.

'Fuck that,' he said. 'She called today,' and, after further denials, 'Let me talk to that shithead of a manager.' But the manager also claimed there was nothing for Rosie.

'She's a decent old dame!' Lennie said. He hadn't had lunch or dinner. 'She needs someplace comfortable to sit. She don't ask for much. Just bring the fucking chair out and we'll call it quits.'

'Let's lose the potty mouth, sir. There are children here.'

'You saying I've got a fucking shitty mouth? That what you fucking saying, dimshit?'

The manager hesitated. The veins in Lennie's neck felt like fire hoses. 'What's your name? Lennie. Take a breath, Lennie. I can't bring you the chair if you don't have a receipt. And maybe this isn't even the store where your wife made the purchase.'

Lennie could picture his fist sending the man's jawbone into the XL Depends, but at the anger-management class, the shrink had encouraged him to think of less violent images. He said he was retraining Lennie's neural synapses, whatever the fuck that meant. So, instead, Lennie made an effort to picture something warm and fluffy. As he pulled out his cell phone to call Rosie, he was picturing teddy bears on a rotisserie spit over six roaring blowtorches.

Reversing out of the parking space, he spun his wheels and came close to trashing the transmission when he slammed his Lincoln Town Car into drive. 'Honey, sweetie, poochie pie,' he muttered to himself. 'Get the fuck out of my way, moron!' he yelled as he cut off another driver on the 95 going south all the way to Miami. What kind of a maniac buys stuff in *Miami*? And doesn't tell you?

It had been a terrible day at work. The boss had decided to donate the contents of the tip jar to a local charity right after his best customer dropped him a sawbuck. He'd taken a half-inch off the top of his thumb on the meat slicer and cauterised the wound on the grill. A woman had come in and held up the whole line talking to her lawyer on her cell phone and, when he'd taken another customer ahead of her, she'd hit him with a goldfish in a plastic bag, before threatening to get him fired for his appalling customer service. He needed the job and he needed to stay out of trouble. All he'd wanted to do after that was go home and eat chocolate popsicles.

And instead, here he was, driving an hour out of his way in peak-hour traffic to pick up a recliner for his crazy old neighbour lady. He hit the button on his air machine and a plastic woman inflated in the passenger seat. The HOV lane was always far less crowded but if he got any more tickets, he'd lose his licence. He'd convinced his kosher mother to eat lobster once, by telling her it was chicken of the sea.

Rosie drove him nuts. She really did. She'd wake up on Friday and think it was Monday, eat her earplugs, then put her swimsuit on upside down, a sight he really could have done without. He'd cut the suit off her, with her wailing that it was her favourite, and him blushing for the first time in sixty years. 'You love me, Lennie. Admit it,' she'd said, in her new fur bikini.

'You're a freakshow,' he said to her. 'A fucking freakshow.'

'But you love me.'

'You're going to get yourself kilt one of these days. Strangled by a push-up bra.'

He didn't want it to be him that walked in and found her dead body still watching *Abortion Clinic,* where you got to see miniature human beings being yanked out of pussies with meat hooks. But it would have been weird to say that, so instead he said, 'Your titties just fell out of your bikini top.'

She washed his dishes every day, and made his bed, and vacuumed the floors. Once, he'd caught her taking the neighbours in to look at his bathroom. 'It's the best bathroom in Century Village,' she said. She'd charged the women a dollar a piece to use the toilet with the rectal blow dryer, and if they wanted to use the walk-in aromatherapy aqua-massage unit, ten. She spent the money buying deodorisers for his place that had names like Peppermint Crush and Sugar Plum Fantasy. Breathing often felt like chewing on a solid stick of chemical air freshener. She'd stolen his spare keys and made copies for fifty of her best friends.

On Sundays, he sat around adding to a list he kept in his wallet: The Sixteen Reasons I Hate You. Number one was

Naked, you look like the cat killed you and coughed you up in a hairball. Number two was *You miss stuff when you vacuum because you won't wear your fucking glasses.* Number three was *When you scratch your ass you get crud under your fingernails.* These, he felt, were more than adequate reasons to hate Rosie. When he saw her lying on her back on the floor, though, all he could think of was how she put plastic flowers in front of his condo too, and sprayed them with Shalimar. She was always nice to him. She was a sweet old lady. He thought about throwing away the list.

She deserved better than him.

But when he gets to Miami and the traffic completely stops, he takes out a pen and opens his wallet and adds a seventeenth reason he hates her.

Seventeen: Tattooing your eyebrows onto your face when you are ninety shows you're whacked right out of your head and you ain't never coming back.

The Miami Target looks the same as every other Target. As if clowns have been buried in the concrete out front and only their noses are sticking up for air. Inside, the manager has an ink stain on his pocket, right where his pen would end, and a tattoo of a butterfly on his wrist. The faggot.

'Are you driving a pick-up truck?' he says.

'Just bring out the fucking recliner, fairy boy,' says Lennie. 'I don't have all day.'

'Why certainly, sir,' says the manager, before he disappears into the back for an hour.

Lennie sees salespeople trotting in and out between the rubber doors and then, after fifty-seven minutes and twelve seconds, when the doors are propped open to let someone through with a piece of patio furniture, he sees the manager dipping a doughnut into a cup of coffee and schmoozing with a young dude in tight Levi's.

The coffee cup hits the overhead sprinkler and showers the stockroom. The doughnut goes down the front of the manager's pants and is stickily involved in the uncomplicated grip Lennie has on the man's balls when he shouts in his face, 'Where's the chair, you fuckwad?'

'Right,' says the manager. 'Over there.' He points at something the size of a dead whale and swathed in plastic.

Lennie steps over and takes a look. Whatever it is, it's strapped to a pallet that is twice as big as his Town Car.

'This can't be it,' he says. Rosie could be dead by now. She could have fallen into the couch and drowned. He's so hungry he could eat this heap of plastic. He could fucking eat his own hand.

'I'm going to be filing a report,' says the manager. 'You're lucky I don't call the cops.'

'How the hell am I going to get this monster home?' Lennie says.

'If you're not out of here in less than a minute,' says the manager.

'You'll what?' says Lennie. Hot barbecued teddy bears. Chunks of little old lady alternated with slabs of fag manager on bamboo skewers. Bone sucking sauce.

'There's a guy over in electronics,' says the manager, 'with a pick-up truck. He charges twenty-five dollars to deliver.'

The pick-up pulls in outside Rosie's apartment a few seconds ahead of Lennie, and he's irked, by god; it's irksome to be beaten to a parking spot by a Mexican. It's already eight o'clock at night and he's imagining Rosie rotting peacefully or at the very least comatose and can't decide if he's happy or not. But then the door opens to his condo and Rosie comes out, leading two women he's never seen before, who are carrying towels and wearing bathrobes.

'I told you you'd love sleeping in his bed,' she's saying. 'That heating pad is something else.' She turns her head and looks at the Mexican. 'Oh you sweetums!' she squeals. 'You brought me my chair!'

'What the fuck?' Lennie says.

Rosie kisses the Mexican's cheek and slips him a hundred dollar tip. 'Oh you big brave man,' she says.

'Stop it, Rosie,' says Lennie. It's a toss-up who he wants to clobber more: Rosie or the Mexican who is now taking the chair off the back of his truck as if it is a kiddy pool instead of an ocean liner.

'You should get some nice manners like this nice man,' she says. 'Just look at those nice muscles.'

Any moment now she'll be planting plastic dahlias in the chico's rear bumper and stealing the keys to his truck. Any moment now Lennie will tear the door off the fucking pick-up and give her a sixty-pound necklace.

'You won't even slip your tongue in,' she shouts at Lennie. There are clusters of old biddies gathering on the sidewalks and the balconies. 'Not even once! Call yourself a man? I bet your schmekkie hasn't worked in years.'

'Rosie!' he yells. 'Shut the fuck up or I'll ...'

'You'll what?' she says. 'You can't even be trusted to bring a chair home. You gotta go hire some Spanish. Come on, buster, watcha gonna do? Hit an old lady?'

'Fight!' calls one of the old dames, and the others pick it up. 'Fight! Fight!'

'I don't need your stupid cleaning,' he says. 'I hate those fucking air fresheners. When I get into my bed it gets messed up anyhow, so why does it need to be made? That condom this morning? I used it on a hooker. She's twenty and her tits are level with her armpits instead of her cunt.'

There is a succulent insuck of breath from all the old women.

'Don't you dare,' says Rosie, her eyelids drooling. 'You ungrateful bastard.' Her hands shake and she fumbles in her pockets.

'You think I'd *ever* put my tongue in your mouth? I'd sooner put it in a dead dog's ass,' Lennie says. 'A dog with worms. And you know what? You owe me for all those times I took you out to Orchid Gardens. That place serves such shit. It's a wonder I haven't died of cancer.'

'Oh yeah,' she says. 'Well, you owe me for all those times I made you soup after your daughter OD'd. You'd still be wearing the same pair of underpants if it wasn't for me.'

'I didn't need your help. I was fine. It's *you* who needs *my* help.'

'If you were fine, how come I had to spoonfeed you?'

'I hate you! I have a list of the seventeen reasons I hate you!' The paper is only halfway out of his wallet when the keys to his condo come whizzing through the night air to cut a triangle out of his right ear and continue on to land amongst the plastic flowers.

A week later, Lennie sits on the toilet in his dark bathroom, his pants around his ankles, the cold ring of the seat numbing his butt and the backs of his legs. He can't sleep. He hasn't been in to work. He has a cough for the first time he remembers. An odd noise rouses him, a sound like a stone cracking a windshield at high speed. A cat? Not exactly. Maybe some flying night thing hit the bathroom window? His ears extend like trumpets. That noise. What was it? And then, a tiny light glows on the tile near the door. The cold, echoing room fills for a second, less than a second, with purple shadows. A moment later, the light blinks on again, halfway to his feet. It's a firefly. A shitty little firefly. He's never seen one so pathetic. It lights up again, right next to his foot this time, wants to drink the piss around the toilet no doubt. The light is ... eerie. There comes again the odd sound. His eyes swivel in the dark. Where is the bastard? The firefly zaps up into his face, batting against his lips, igniting the air directly in front of his eyes, before crashing against the gleam of his eyeball. 'Fuck!' The many legs of the thing swarming over his skin, tangling in his eyelashes. 'Aaaaa!' He jumps up and staggers against the sink, having forgotten the pants around his ankles. The firefly an inch in front of his mouth, the long brown body, the red ball connecting it to the tiny black head, the sad, sorry, fuckuselessness of it, lights a bright circle in midair and then flies straight up into his nostril.

He paws at his face, lurches across the room and runs his head into the wall. 'Get out,' he shouts. 'Get the fuck out of my life! I don't need you.' He fumbles for the switch. A sick green glow from the fluorescent strip fills the space. On the tiles lays the firefly. Its wings are outlined in yellow. They are in several pieces. The bug is a mess. He waits for it to light up, for some movement, but there is nothing. He finds himself waiting. Waiting. His breath held. The cold air still. The light it made could not have come from this small of a thing.

He steps into his pants and pulls them up. Lays a square of toilet paper over the firefly. 'Fuck you,' he says. 'As if I care.'

Everything You Always Wanted to Know

Marvelous Lemonjello sits in a café in Paris, France, with his long-term partner, Andy Melrose. Marvel lifts his camera, preparing to shoot his lover. Andy hunches over the tiny white cup of espresso, his blond hair covering his face. Marvel no longer has hair. A surfeit, he is told, of testosterone. His barber encouraged him to completely shave his head when the bald patch resembled the Soviet Union. His head gets cold now, and even in spring he has to wear a dorky knit cap. Like an old man. Which he absolutely isn't. Fifty-four is middle aged. Andy just had his thirty-fifth birthday. This trip is – in fact – the birthday gift.

Marvel reaches into his pocket and slides from his chair to kneel on the filthy flagstones at Andy's feet.

'Not here!' hisses Andy, panicking. He hates when Marvel makes it obvious they are a couple. What do the young people call it these days? PDAs. Public Displays of Affection.

'Andy,' says Marvel, plopping a jewellery box on Andy's knee. 'Will you marry me?'

Andy folds his arms across his chest and looks away. He snaps his fingers under cover of his cashmere-covered elbows.

This gesture goes through Marvel like a circular saw, spitting out bone and gristle, little bits of his brain and heart and bowels hitting the pressed-tin ceiling like shot, landing in other patrons' cups of cappuccino. *Plink plink.*

He is older than Andy, and dare he say it, wiser too. Wealthier. More masculine. He has more cats. That alone ought to count for something. He's always wanted to be the one who asked, who snuck out to get the ring, the guy down on his knees in a puddle of coffee and emotion, madly in love, in Paris, in a chic little café, on a delicate, light-filled spring morning. He knows it's a bit late for all that, but he *wants* it to be true.

A street-cleaning truck roars by and a fish skeleton flies up from under the brushes and hits the wooden doorframe of the café with a sharp *tchack*, and then hangs there, trembling, somehow suspended from two splinters of bone that are jammed into the wood.

He shudders and his left eye twitches.

'Excuse,' says the waiter, returning with the bill. 'Is your Papa okay?' he says to Andy.

Marvel tugs at Andy's hand and tries to slide the ring onto his finger. It doesn't fit. Of course. Marvel has always been terrible at details. When Andy jerks his hand away, the waiter asks, 'Is this gentleman bothering you?'

'No,' says Andy, but then he turns to Marvel. 'Not here! Can't you get *anything* right?'

Marvel stands. 'This is such bullshit,' he says. Snaps the box shut. Remembers again the photograph of the old man at the Pride parade. He leans down and kisses Andy hard, on the lips, mouth open. PDA. Public Display of Aggression. 'I'm going home.' He knows he does not mean the boutique hotel on the Left Bank, or even his apartment in Boys' Town, but his mother's house in Avalanche, Wisconsin. Where there are mice and manure and people who will love him forever. He vomits a little defeat into his mouth and swallows it down.

Marvel's been waiting all these years for Andy to grow into the mature partner he needs. He's endured hundreds, no, *thousands* of people, saying, 'Is this your son?' He's patiently sat through the bar-hopping phase, the alternate-piercings phase, and the open-relationship phase, waiting, waiting, waiting for when Andy could officially be declared old enough for him. Friends had made jokes about NAMBLA and Marvel had flinched.

Now, on Marvel's way out of the café, he turns to inspect the fish skeleton hanging on the doorframe. It stinks. Marvel can't believe no one else notices the odour. He wants to cry. But truthfully, he isn't really into Public Displays of Anything. Including tears.

Marvelous Lemonjello crouches under the dining room table, a book tucked between his legs. *Everything You Always Wanted to Know About Sex (But Were Afraid to Ask).* He's almost worn out the chapter on homosexuality. Large parts of it dart through his mind at inopportune times. He is thirteen. He has a hard-on every afternoon at four o'clock.

Twenty-nine years later, he finds a copy of the book on a table at the Brandeis Used Book Sale. The book smells faintly of lube and, turning it over, he sees again the doctor, the *professional* who wrote it. What, exactly, is under that trench coat? Trench coats are like kilts. They make him curious.

He glances right and left, then opens the book to the chapter he was obsessed with as a teenage boy, completely unable to remember a word of it.

> *Couldn't homosexuals just be born that way? A lot of homosexuals would like to think so. They prefer*

to consider their problem the equivalent of a club foot or a birthmark; just something to struggle through life with.

What the fuck? The man, Marvelous Lemonjello, over-certified art therapy professional and concert harmonicist, forty-two years old, thrusts the book from him, angry and blushing, thirteen years old again. No wonder there is a whole generation of gay men dragging their sorry-assed selves to his practice. He sees now that all those forgotten passages have been dripping into his veins like a life-long transfusion of toxic shame. *Club foot.*

Fuck. No wonder he can't get a boyfriend.

The Sunday before he met Andy for the first time, Marvelous visited his friend, Apricot. She rented a run-down Victorian in Roger's Park. The dusty windows let in a little drugged light that slurred and staggered all over Apricot as she lay on the couch with her lover, Squishy. They were rubbing each other's feet with an eroticism that seemed entirely misguided. It was indecent, but who was he to say? Marvel dropped into a straight-backed chair near a dead geranium.

'Do you know if you can use Botox on places other than your face?' he asked. 'I mean, does the "tox" mean it's toxic?' He clutched his hands tightly together so he would not inadvertently give away the location he had in mind.

'The person who you end up living with for the rest of your life isn't going to love you for your body, Marvelo,' said Apricot. 'He's going to love you for your mind. Your heart. You have such a big aura. Someone has *got* to notice that.'

Squishy sat up a little and said, 'They'll probably love you for that ass of yours too. Someone's got to notice that. You should buy tighter jeans, Marv.'

Apricot stopped rubbing. 'Shut up, Squishy. Marvelo needs to be philosophical about this. He needs some healing around the whole age thing.' Her skin, at forty, looked ploughed by a drunken Amishman.

'Can we not talk about this with Squishy here? It's ...' Marvel squirmed in his chair. He ripped off some of the dead leaves from the geranium and waved them in the air. '... embarrassing. I'm not remotely interested in the way either of you view my ass.'

'Go make some tea, Squishy. Go.' Apricot shoved her lover's legs off the couch. 'You know what, Marvelo? I saw an ad in the personals yesterday that you might be interested in.'

'Oh God. I hate gay men.'

'Sure you do, sugarbutt.'

'You're *not* funny.'

'Aw, Marvel. You've lost your sense of humour. Ever since your fortieth birthday, everything is too serious to laugh at. Here. I got the ad from the *Windy City Times*. It's funny. Really.' She threw him the paper.

'Jesus, this has got to be the *most* depressing bible of human loneliness on the planet.'

'Not to mention kinkiness. Check out the fourth one from the top. *White-out!* That's what I call imaginative!' Suddenly she was the expert on what was kinky. He frowned. Where had his friend gone, the one who made tasteless British food and wore a chunky hand-knit sweater that looked like a llama had died on her shoulders?

'Here it is ... *I would like to dedicate this ad to my mother (narcissistic burlesque dancer, 78) who is responsible for me being an anal retentive, straight-acting, self-hating gay man at 42. Man. 42. Almost single. You too? Join me.* Isn't that great? He sounds just like you!'

Marvel didn't move or respond. There was a long silence.

'Jesus! It *is* you!'

That night, after he'd cried for an hour or so in his bathroom, he'd spotted the review for a new bar on Yahoo.

Ramrod, Halsted St, Chicago
I agree with the other reviewers, that Ramrod has some serious flaws. The crowd tends to be fat and middle-aged. Their speakers are tinny pieces of crap and the music is smooth rock, if you can believe that. The shirtless bartenders should spare us the gory vision. Those hypocrites made their patio non-smoking. They sell alcohol and I've bought weed there almost every weekend. I personally think the manager, a former smoker, is just being a dick.

It had sounded like his kind of crowd.

So the next Friday night, Marvelous tries out the new bar. In one corner there's a writers' group going on. A guy with a small waist and a ponytail and Levi 501s looks his way and then looks again.

Marvelous checks the man out in the mirror several times, before heading for the pool table. Ponytail hands a sheaf of papers to the guy he's standing next to and walks towards Marvelous, not exactly looking at him but not looking away either. Marvelous mimes sliding a pool cue between his fingers. Despite his strong instinct to run, run, as fast as he can, Marvel summons his muscles to smile. The overhead lights flicker.

'Manhattan?' Marvelous asks his new friend later, after completely routing him at pool.

'Jack Daniels, straight up,' the man replies, all trailer park butch. Andy. His name is Andy. Their hips bump in the crowd. The first time accidentally. Andy runs his hand back through his hair and tightens the rubber around his ponytail. Marvel gets a whiff of Irish Spring, clean sweat, something yeasty and delicious drifting from Andy's armpits.

'Uh,' Marvelous says. His stomach rumbles. 'I'm working on some Debussy. Would you like to come back and hear it?' He doesn't mention that he plays Debussy on harmonica.

'I have perfect pitch, you know,' says Andy as they walk towards Marvel's apartment. Marvel would like to take Andy's hand, but he thinks it might be too forward. He hasn't held a man's hand in years. They pass the park where only last night a man sprang from the swing and groped Marvel, panting, 'I want to have my way with you.'

'Get off me,' Marvel had said then, shoving the man away. 'I need to get to know you a *little*, you know. Haven't you ever heard of a *relationship*?'

'Jee-sus!' the man had said, 'You old queens make me puke. Listen man, I seen you walking home alone for about two years now. Can't you tell a mercy fuck when you see one?'

Old queen? Forty-two isn't old. But these days, standing in a bar, hardly anyone looks his way. *Look at me look at me look at me for godsakes look at me.* 'I'm a human being!' he wants to shout. 'Deserving of love!'

'What's wrong?' asks Andy, squeezing Marvel's hand.

'Don't you believe me?'

Marvel can't remember what it was that he was supposed to believe. 'Of course I do,' he says.

Although it turns out that Andy doesn't, after all, have perfect pitch.

Sometimes Marvelous secretly wondered if he was a lesbian. It would certainly make things a lot easier. Unlike most of his friends, he wanted a relationship that lasted for forty years, or until he died and his lover came on Sundays to cover his grave with red roses. He'd wanted Andy to move in right away and told him the joke that Apricot had told him: What do lesbians bring on the second date? A U-Haul. It wasn't funny. It was true. At least, for him. He still couldn't believe his good fortune that this wonderful man, Andy, young, beautiful, witty, wanted to live with him. The night that Andy actually came round with a U-Haul and they carried the boxes in and lined them up against the dining room wall was one of the best nights of his life. Andy sat on the edge of the bed, their shared bed now, and bounced gently. 'I never thought I'd find someone like you,' he said. And Marvelous thought he meant someone kind and gentle and clever and handsome, but now, sometimes, in his worst moods, he thought maybe Andy had simply meant wealthy.

They worked from his home for years, him painting with clients in his sun-filled front office, Andy creating huge canvasses on the glassed-in back porch, so that the smell of turpentine lingered all through the apartment and he could taste it in the back of his throat when he ate Andy's rice and tofu stir-fries. Sometimes, new clients asked him about the monumental murals on his walls and he smiled to think that they didn't know Andy. Who could not know Andy? His slender neck bent over his work, pale and tender, like a bean sprout, inviting caresses. The huffs and luffs as he manoeuvered bigger pieces of work down the back stairs. The way they washed dishes together after supper, Andy snapping the wet towel at his legs, moving closer and closer to him, leaning against him, so that all their movements moved the other man too.

How they laughed when, one day, Marvel said, 'If I find out there's a heaven after I die, and all my friends who got AIDS are in it having a gay old time, I'm going to kill myself.' It became their inside joke. *If I find out there's a heaven.* The truth was something he'd never said to Andy. He'd felt, all these years, that he'd somehow stumbled into heaven and the door to his earlier, lonely days had closed quietly behind him.

'We can't be late,' Andy says, the night before Pride. It's a month until his thirty-fifth birthday and a couple of days before their twelfth anniversary. Andy's been rootling through the cupboards in search of hidden presents. But, unlike in previous years, Marvel feels uninspired, present-wise.

'Why not? It's not like *I'm* getting the lifetime achievement award.'

'We're not talking about you here, Marvel.'

Sometimes Andy drives Marvel crazy: he's a stickler for protocol, always worrying what people will think. That he ever agreed to go out with Marvel is one of the wonders of the modern world. 'There's a rule,' he'd said, 'for how old a person has to be in order to date them. It's half your age plus seven.' Marvel had done the math. Andy had been, was still, too young for him to date.

'You have the tiniest hands, you know,' says Andy now. It was one of the first compliments Andy had ever said to him and still had the power to evoke that earlier intense phase of their relationship, when people they knew avoided them because they'd been embarrassing to watch. He smiles to hear it now. 'Hands like a woman.' *Like a woman.* Marvel knows it's a sentence from that bloody book. *Everything You Always Wanted to Know.* He knows it and yet he's completely defenceless.

'I meant it as a compliment,' says Andy later, to the icy car. 'Your skin is so soft.'

Marvelous drives without blinking. If he closes his eyes even once, even for a moment, he's going to cry. Will his eyes get so dry that his eyelids get stuck open, like sometimes happens to his top lip when his teeth dry out? Would that warrant a trip to the emergency room? What do desiccated eyeballs look like? Will prune eyes make his twitch worse? Who will put roses on his grave?

Andy lays his hand on Marvel's arm. 'You're beautiful, you know. Just the way you are.' As if all this is about is their age difference, Marvel's wrinkles and grey hairs and love handles. Andy offers up this comment whenever he thinks Marvel is feeling decrepit. It used to make Marvel feel better for a day or two but now it's passed into the realm of meaningless comments like 'Have a nice day' and 'I love you'. His left eye twitches again and he glances in the rear-view mirror to make sure that his sclera isn't dehydrating. Andy's face is turned away. He mutters, 'I meant it as a compliment' and something that sounds like 'oversensitive'.

At the awards dinner, they sit near the front, masticating the chicken Kiev in silence even though it's absolutely not part of their macrobiotic diet. When the MC stands up to announce Shepsel Lunkowicz, pioneer gay activist, they lay down their forks and look around. An old man, Shepsel probably, pushes his walker down the central aisle. The hind legs of the walker are covered with split tennis balls. Someone drops his spoon and the clink as it hits his plate sounds abnormally loud.

Shepsel reaches the dais and frowns at the three steps. He can't quite lift his foot as high as the first step and his shoe hits the edge repeatedly, with a sound like a head hitting a wooden beam. There are snickers from the back of the room. A fly falls into Marvel's wine glass and drowns.

There's no railing. Shepsel kneels briefly to steady himself. Breathy sounds of exertion break the absolute and appalling silence. There are two dirty streaks on the knees of his white dress pants and he bats at them with his paws and staggers a little. The MC puts out his hand to catch the honoree and, as he does so, glances quickly but obviously at his own watch, and then there are outright laughs and a shudder of applause.

It is only later that Marvel wonders why no one in all that huge crowd didn't stand to help the old man. It is only then that he wonders why *he* didn't stand.

The next day, at the Pride parade, which Marvelous always wants to boycott but which Andy insists they attend, Andy takes photos of horrified farm parents standing abandoned in the crowd, their grey faces slack with shock. Andy holds his camera, watching for the precise moment when the float bearing Taj Mahal passes by, trailing clouds of glory and expensive perfume, for the moment when the spackled old man and his haggard wife see their son in feathers and rainbow glitter and a bra, and he presses the shutter exactly then.

'You've got to stop that,' says Marvel. 'It's abusive.'

'It's art.'

'It's hateful. Drag queens aren't who we are.'

Andy looks at him and his lip rises so that the brittle light hits his canine teeth. 'The world is bigger than when you came out, Marvel. There's all types of folks under the queer umbrella now.'

'Oh, so now I'm some old fogey who had a lobotomy back in the fifties.'

'That's not what I was saying.'

'What were you saying then?'

'It doesn't matter. Whatever it was, you'll turn it into a criticism of you.'

Andy lifts the camera and aims it at Marvelous. 'You have such an odd look on your face right now. Hold still. No one ever need know you aren't here for your son.'

'Yes,' says Marvelous Lemonjello, as the flash explodes in his face. 'You're right.'

The photo in the gallery is labelled *Old Man in Chinos.*

When Marvelous manages to get Andy off to one side, he asks, 'Who makes up the titles for your photos?' and Andy, a little drunk on the free wine and the success of his show, says, 'Me. Why?'

Old Man in Chinos. Marvel is wearing those same chinos now and he wipes his hands on them. 'I'm going home,' he says. 'I'm not feeling so well.'

At home, on the computer, he looks up airfares to Paris, romantic hotels, wedding rings. He pulls out his credit card without thought, even as he browses Manhunt, the sad pickings, mostly straight men. His cat jumps up onto his shoulder, her claws seeming to hook right under his scapular. It's 2 a.m. Andy must have forgotten where he lives with this *old man in chinos.* Marvelous wanders the apartment, shutting windows, pushing the cat away from his feet. The proposal, he thinks, will be beautiful.

If You Cut Off Her Head, a Horse Falls Out

Madison stepped out of the smoke, her long hair writhing around her face in the roaring forewind. The bushfire was still some distance away, but here, ahead of the flames, it was ten degrees hotter than it had been back at her farm. When she shut the truck door, the hot metal raised a line of blisters along her thumb.

'Porky!' she called. Then, quieter, 'Dad?'

On the way to the national park, she'd told her daughter to get down on the floor and stare at the rubber matting if Porky turned nasty and came at them with a gun. 'I'm shitting meself, Mum,' Olivia said, almost a teenager. Sarcastic.

'You should be,' Madison said, and there was something in her eyes and something in the razor edge to her voice that finally got through to Olivia. Now Madison heard the click of the door lock on the truck even over the shrieking of the wind and the panicked screams of the cockatoos. A dugite slithered by, right under her feet and she shuddered.

'Dad!'

Madison ran a wildlife shelter on her farmland. She fed shearers, and deloused dogs, and drove long distances with dead animals dripping in the tray of the truck, and she taped corellas' wings and carried abandoned joeys in sheepskin pouches she slung around her neck. She worked hard and was proud of her strength.

She avoided family functions, but Olivia was curious and looked through the mail for news from Madison's two sisters, Selena and Euryale. Olivia went to boarding school down in Perth during the school year, and she thought Madison should find out more about the family while records were still available. But Madison didn't want to. The subject, frankly, made her skin crawl.

Her husband Frank warned her when they'd bought land in Badgingarra that Porky squatted about twenty kilometres north of them, in the Watheroo National Park. He said they didn't have to live that close to her father. They could buy land elsewhere. But Madison knew that the land in Badgingarra was cheap and readily available. Near the coast, rainfall was more likely and the man was twenty kilometres away, so she shrugged and they bought the block.

People gossiped about Porky in town, but no one knew of their connection. Once, Madison had been parked at the servo, filling her car with petrol, when she heard the tail end of some man ranting on the radio. He'd been going off about the government's tolerance of Asian immigrants, and how flat-headed foreigners were stealing the bread out of decent Australians' mouths and she'd thought, 'What a nutjob,' and then the announcer said, 'Thanks for that Porky, but I'm going to have to take another caller.' Her face turned red and sweat broke out all over her body, and she looked around, afraid that everyone knew she was related to him, that there was a flashing neon sign on the roof of her car announcing that she was lunatic Porky's daughter.

After that, she avoided even driving past the national park on her way to somewhere else. She dropped the wallet containing her last photo of Porky into the dam. And she asked

Frank not to bring her news about her father: it just made her unhappy.

This was not, however, the first time she'd driven up the dirt track to his squat. A few months before the fire, she'd passed his ancient Harley outside the Badgingarra pub, and then, unthinking, driven to where Frank had said Porky lived, in a humpy hidden deep within the park. But she couldn't find the house and she wasn't going to go back to look again. She shouldn't have gone in the first place.

And now, here she was, for the second time, standing in the national park, on an errand to find her father. When they'd seen the bushfire, the direction it was heading, she'd pressed Frank for detailed instructions to Porky's place. Frank couldn't go, though he wanted to; he was busy wetting down their home paddocks and the tin roof of their house.

The bushfire was only a few miles away now. It was hot enough to fry eggs on the dashboard, hotter in the forewind than she'd ever experienced, and she'd grown up in the country near Fitzroy Crossing, lived through deadly summer after deadly summer. The grass trees shimmied in the heat and smoke rose from them. They were in danger of spontaneous combustion. The air smelled like cat piss and barbecued lamb and was full of tiny rips of colour: burning embers. Her bare arms were covered in white blisters. The sun's mouth hung open and a black lick of sunlight fell through the smoke.

Walking towards Porky's capsizing house, she felt sick and dizzy and afraid. Half-eaten skeletons of some small animal lay scattered around the yard, their bleached spines arching out of the red sand. One had a long ginger striped tail and she saw that it was a cat. Had been a cat. She had the heaves.

Madison's feet sweated in her thongs. In all the years she'd lived in the bush, she never got used to shoes. She went barefoot unless it was summer and even then only wore thongs because the sand was too hot to stand on without getting third-degree burns. She never wore make-up, carried kangaroo droppings in the front pockets of her jeans, and her unbrushed hair jutted from her head.

Porky's house was made of grey weatherboard that had, perhaps, once been painted black. Curls of paint fell off as she watched. The fire, when it arrived, would eat the frangible wood in a second. One side, where the door used to be, had collapsed. Did Porky climb in through a window? And where was he? Closer, it seemed that thousands of sheets of newspaper had been torn and wadded into the walls and that was what caused them to swell and bulge as they did. But from these swollen places, even above the howl of the wind, rose a low zuzzing, and, horrified, she saw that the walls formed a massive hive, that the house itself was alive with bees, and what she had earlier thought was flaking paint on the weatherboard was actually a shifting coat of black bees.

Madison drove down to Perth to see Dr Idle on Wednesdays, and though he encouraged her to talk about her father, she couldn't. Dr Idle thought she'd be able to eventually, and he told Frank that Madison was doing much better. The kangaroo shit in her pockets was not a serious concern and neither was the ever increasing number of burns on her arms.

'At least she feels things,' the doctor said. 'That's a step in the right direction.'

Privately, he told Madison that if she continued burning her arms he would have to report it, and she'd end up in Graylands again, with the crazies. She'd barked at him then, and flapped her invisible crazy wings, and slobbered a little, but underneath, she'd been afraid. She'd stopped putting the iron on her arms a couple of weeks before the bushfire.

Graylands was where she'd been sent when her mum died. At Katie's funeral, Madison began walking backwards and couldn't make herself stop. She'd walked backwards from the cemetery at Wongan Hills, out the gate, down the hill, through the farm machinery dealership and out the other side of town. She'd been picked up by a Poseidon Fisheries truck driver on the road, miles from anywhere, her lips blistered a bright bubblegum pink. She'd still been walking backwards, and he'd tied her to the door handle with a bit of rope until he could get her some help. 'Good luck, dolly,' he said, when he handed her over to the police. He gave her a packet of cigarettes and a box of matches from the roadhouse up in Roebourne. She didn't smoke.

Frank had been her roommate at Graylands except he'd been Francie back then. His parents sent him down to the booby hatch because he was convinced he was a boy. Everyone else was convinced of it too.

The nurses called Francie to change their spark plugs and plunge the toilets and lift heavy boxes and he did all these things with a smile. Francie held the door open for Madison and called her Miss Mooshy and at night, when Madison missed her mum, let her lean against his chest and drip her nose all over his nice white shirt. He held her head there, very gently, and stroked her curious hair. He gave her a necklace of coral from the Red Sea and a tiny flag of Sicily. After Francie officially changed his gender, they married and took up farming land in the wheatbelt and no one in the district had been any the wiser.

Frank was a good farmer, a good husband, a terrific lover and – best of all – knew how to keep a secret.

They were both doing well now. They didn't even drink Coca-Cola because they heard it messed with your moods or did something weird to your endocrine system. Olivia, of course, wasn't Frank's child. Madison wasn't really sure whose child Olivia was, because there'd been that time when she was walking backwards and she didn't remember anything from then. She certainly didn't remember anything that might have caused a Olivia to happen. It might have been the truck driver. Frank thought it was. Madison had wanted to have more children with Frank but she couldn't stay pregnant. Not for lack of trying.

'Do you ever think about killing him?' Dr Idle said.

'No. Yes. Sometimes.'

Madison hid her hands in the cracks between the leather seat cushions. She kicked the box of tissues at her feet. The jarrah floorboards were highly polished and reflected an amplified version of Madison's red thongs.

'I would,' said Dr Idle. 'I'd imagine gory deaths for him, if I was you.'

But he wasn't, of course. He wasn't her. He had no other queer clients. He had never met a transgender person until Frank came into the office one day to go out to lunch with Madison. The doctor tried his best to be open-minded and non-judgemental and all those good things that shrinks are supposed to be, but still, he kept on calling Frank 'she'. He referred to them as a lesbian couple. He winced when Madison said that Frank was considering getting pregnant himself. When he was uncomfortable, he crossed and recrossed his legs. Some days, he looked like a three year old who needed to pee.

'I went to see his house a while back,' Madison said, 'but I couldn't find it.'

'That's very Freudian.'

'What do you mean?'

The doctor hesitated. 'You've never told me what Porky looks like.'

'Thin. Bearded. Dark red skin with a massive crop of malignancies. Singlet and shorts. Unwashed. Tattoos of machinery parts on his calves. Swastikas.'

'Beautiful.'

'Not.' Madison tried to turn her mind away from the image she had of Porky standing in the Badgingarra laundromat, shaking the small Vietnamese owner by his shirtfront. The man's lips opening and closing. Spit launched out of his mouth. Contrails of saliva. If she lingered with that image too long, the words to the scene would return. The smell of the freshly washed jeans. Hot towels. Wet shirts.

'You fucker! Get out of my country! No one wants you here! Yer a leech, that's what!'

Porky's back was facing Madison, and the owner looked over her father's shoulder toward her, pleading for help with his eyes.

'Dad,' she said.

'What the fuck do *you* want?' he asked, whirling around.

'Let him go,' she said, her fists curling into balls. Porky looked sideways at the image of her reflected in the shiny fronts of the washing machines. She was full of muscle. Her hair, alone, looked like something dangerous.

He shoved the Vietnamese man towards the door. 'Fuck off, you wanker.'

That day was the first time she'd seen Porky in ten years and she didn't know what to say to him. How are you? No matter what she thought of, it wouldn't be what she really wanted to say. She thought about complimenting him on his small bike trailer, a sofa chair on wheels with a cushion that flipped up to reveal a toilet underneath. But by the time she'd got her words in order, Porky had left and she'd lost another twenty minutes of her life. She walked out of the laundromat backwards, saw herself in the dusty window, and stopped.

A half-hour later, though, her heart still felt like a possum was rootling around in the chambers. She was breathless and clammy and what little she could see appeared at the end of a black tube much like a telescope, but in reverse.

Porky was an old man, really. He couldn't fight his way out of a wet paper bag. He was crepey and grey and crumbling in the toothsome. He'd lost most of his hair and he smelled bad. He'd need secateurs to trim his toenails. It irked her that she was afraid of him.

'Yer bloody lucky there's so much smoke today or them bees'd have been on ya. They woulda eaten you for breakfast.'

In the rising wind, holding her hair in two bunches at the sides of her head, Madison panted. Her tongue felt as vast and dry as the continent.

Porky laughed. He smacked the side of the house with his hand. A few bees flew into the air and resettled.

'They're sleepy, they are,' he said.

'It's a fire.' She spoke loudly. He looked down at the ground. 'Coming this way. Fast.'

'Really?' he said. 'A fire?' Burning embers rained from the sky. 'What made you think that?'

'Frank said I should come to warn you,' Madison said, realising that this was not the truth; that she had wanted, for some reason, to save her father. 'You're right in its path.'

Porky rolled his eyes. 'Naa,' he said. 'I'm not.'

'You are,' Maddie said. 'You definitely are. No matter what you say.'

'What's the risk?' he said.

'Getting burnt alive.'

'That all? I'd rather be barbecued in me own dear hovel than fried in that tin can of yours.' He jerked his head towards the truck. 'Your bastard doesn't look too happy.'

She meant to say, 'Well then. Be my guest. Burn in hell,' but turning, she saw that Olivia was slimy with sweat, falling out of the truck door, retching. She'd never been good in the heat.

'Betta get her outta here,' the old man, her father, said. 'I'll be orright. The Devil takes care of his own.'

When Madison was growing up, Porky did all of the work around their farm himself. This was not merely to save money – though he was a man who rinsed out the same rubbish bag each time after he'd emptied it and picked up other people's toothpicks from the street to reuse after dinner – but because he believed that other men were spying on his women folk. 'They're a bunch of yobbos,' he said of everyone else, all the millions of people in the world. 'Nothing between the ears except sawdust and stuffing. Nothing intelligent between the legs either.'

Madison and her sisters had helped their mother as much as possible when Porky ran off on benders. They'd paint and clean and nail and hope that he wouldn't notice when he returned. They passed off new furniture as stuff they'd found at the rubbish tip and they passed off new paint as seasonal changes in the quality of the sun. The turquoise wall in the kitchen was because of the winter solstice. In regular light it would look like the white wall it really was.

Other families in Fitzroy Crossing had dads who were a little touched. It was a small country town. It was hot up there pretty much all the time. If the sun could cook an egg, it could probably cook a brain. Those things happened. The local peeping tom was greeted with a cup of tea and instructions to get orf home now, Daryl, love. The man who got his daughter pregnant, not once but twice, was the policeman for the district. His wife did a brisk trade in a shed outside town that had been fitted with an air conditioner and a king-sized bed. So Madison and her sisters learned not to complain. They learned to be grateful that Porky had steady work and kept his hands in his own pockets and didn't go round looking in people's windows at night while they slept.

When Maddie was eight or ten or fourteen, she thought her dad was a bit like one of the sheep that emerged from the bush after a year in the wild. Some of them were salvageable, but the ones that had been fly-struck had to be knocked on the head with a bloody great stone. The ones with half-rotted legs and oozy bum juice and maggots cavorting in their hindquarters. The ones that would fall apart if you touched them. Her dad usually seemed salvageable. But, like even the cleanest of those wild sheep, she preferred him at a distance.

Katie, her mum, had grey hair, a tight little cloche of it clamped on her head. She was short and dumpy and pale and freckled. She was always certain and often right. She'd taught grade one before she got married and she still did, as a substitute, when Porky disappeared for more than a few weeks and left them without money. Porky called her The Gorgon, and she called him Porky because he was so thin and the name stuck. Maddie knew they'd had sex at least three times because there were the three of them, the sisters, to show for it, but it was hard to imagine her lizardlike dad and her steelwool scrubbie mum touching each other, much less getting it on. Still, her parents could have been anything behind closed doors. She didn't really know them.

The family was digging the vegie beds on their farm near Fitzroy Crossing one Sunday. It wasn't the soil or the climate or the rainfall to grow vegies. They did it anyway. Porky insisted. Katie said they might drive into town and buy some cold lemonades if they finished the job before sundown, but Porky said they could make lemonade cheaper and better themselves. Euryale lay on the ground with her head on a stone because she had trouble with the female plumbing.

'I heard,' said Katie, 'that the teachers are all going off on a strike because they want another pay rise.'

Maddie didn't care. She stepped down on her shovel, lifted the hardpan and flipped it over.

'Call themselves teachers? Ha! Not even a dingo leaves its young. And now teachers are set to walk off the job?' Katie said.

Porky laid aside the sack of manure he was dragging and leaned on his shovel. 'What did you say?' he asked. There was a sudden quiet. The girls held their breath.

'Down in Perth, teachers are walking off the job,' Katie said, that's all she said, but the fur lifted on Maddie's arms and she looked up quickly, into Porky's face. Euryale stood up and the three girls moved a few steps away. Something popped in the bushes. Euryale startled and, to cover it, began to kick at the stone she'd been lying on.

'I wouldn't. I'd stay there with them kids and make sure they were learning, no matter if I got paid or not.' Sometimes Katie didn't know when to shut up.

'You'd do that?' said Porky, drawing the shovel slowly out of the dirt with a sound as if the earth itself was hushing her.

Maddie saw the snake where it lay coiled around the rock, like a shadow between the ground and the granite. Euryale hadn't noticed it while she was resting. None of them had. But now Maddie saw it lift its head at her sister's kicking. She knew that her father was about to hit her mother, probably with the flat of the shovel. Her father thought the solution to wrong-headed thoughts was purely physical. He'd never read one of those self-help books about managing your anger or releasing your inner leprechaun or being the change you wanted to see, although he'd developed his own version of that last bit of wisdom. If something rose out of its place in the world, he'd thump it until it fell back in. He'd hit Katie in a movement so fast and so graceful he could have been a ballet dancer. He'd probably think he was doing her a favour. He was generous with his favours in a way that he was not generous with his cash.

Maddie wasn't sure why what her mother had said was wrong. She could see one tiny white cloud away near the horizon at the same time as the snake and her father and Euryale and she could hear the sound of her heart in her ears and the call of the twenty-eights up in the trees and the ragged sound of Selena's breathing right next to her. But she couldn't hear on one side, Euryale's side, because her father had favoured her some time ago with that same shovel. Being a little off-balance made her body more uncertain about things. She wasn't sure that Porky was going to smack the steel of that shovel up against the side of her mother's head. Maybe she was just remembering the way the shovel danced from hand to hand right before it sank into the skin and bone behind her ear. It might have had nothing to do with her mother at all. She stepped backwards. One step. Two. She could see it coming. She thought she could and that made it true. She could see it coming the way rubbish lifting from the floor of the desert presaged rain.

'You'd be a scab, would you?' said Porky. His voice got quieter and quieter and the shovel danced. 'Me own flesh and blood'd be a scab?'

Maddie thought her mother was a queer old bat. She was ashamed of the floral bloomers her mum made for her on the treadle machine and longed for the sleek bikinis that hid at the back of the local drygoods shop. But lying in her bed at night, the sound of the treadle machine and her mother's eternal humming of 'God Save the Queen' and the *schrick* of the shears through the material and the squeak of the floorboards when Katie crept in to lay some bloomerly creation at the end of Maddie's bed, all that was what she imagined on nights when she couldn't sleep. Her mother's smell of mothballs and Velvet soap. The way she *almost* put her lips on Maddie's forehead when she kissed her on those nights, the faintest puff of air as her lips closed together, some sense of human warmth, skin *almost* touching skin, and then the floorboards, the door, the humming.

If she'd been asked if she loved her mother she would have said an automatic yes and then wondered for days if it were true. Or true in the ordinary sense. And what did it matter after all? Love didn't change a thing in her life.

She thought she saw the snake move again and she called out, 'Dad! Look!' but he never looked at her except sometimes, sideways, when he thought she didn't notice.

It was bad, of course. The shouts came loud and fast. I'm not a scab. I couldn't just abandon children, she said. You'd cross a picket line? he said. I would, she said and patted herself on the bosom. I bloody well would. There's a snake, Maddie said. A king brown. The poisonous kind. She might not have said it. It was like the dreams you have where a hag comes and sits on your chest and you scream but nothing comes out of your mouth. She was watching her father's shovel, the way the sun made a sharp white line on the outside edge of the steel blade, the way the tape holding the wooden handle together winked in the light. The truth of what was said and what was not said was impossible to discover. What kind of person are you? Porky said or didn't say.

'I'm a mother. I care about children before me own bloody throat.'

'Since when?' he said. 'You call burnt toast caring about children? You call *being a scab* caring about children?'

The snake zagged across the upended earth toward Maddie. The raised voices had disturbed it. The kicking had set it off. Her sisters moved their eyes from the snake to their father and back again, not knowing which one to watch. Maddie lifted her own shovel and aimed it towards the snake's head.

'Shut up.'

'Who are you telling to shut up?'

The snake opened its mouth to strike. Her father lifted his shovel above his head. Her mother, finally, fell silent.

'Dad,' Madison said, a little while later. She held the decapitated snake's head in her hand as it spasmodically opened and shut its jaws.

It was so very hot. And yet there was Porky wrapping her mother in his shirt. Tucking it in around her throat.

'Fuck off,' he said. She could barely hear him. He did not turn to look at her as she came closer.

'Look at me, Dad,' she said. 'Will you bloody well look at me for once?'

'She's not waking up,' he said. 'She must be really tired.'

But her mother would wake up. Of this Maddie was sure.

'I'll get her a cuppa tea.' He mimed lifting a cup and drinking.

'Dad! Will you just *look*?'

He still crouched over her mother. 'Can't you see I'm flat out here? Yer mother's feeling poorly.'

A little pinkish greyish froth, the colour of fairy floss, leaked from the gorge in Katie's head.

'Have you put on the kettle?'

He bent lower and did not turn even when she slammed the open snake jaw down onto his arm. The snake bit again and again. Two drops of blood fell onto the earth. A horse shrieked from the home paddock. Blood is life. It can be resurrection.

'I can't abide a scab,' he said, but already his voice was blurred. 'She was deliberately riling me up.'

'She never knew when to stop,' he said.

Maybe because the snake was already dead it hadn't killed him. Oh, he'd been sick all right. He'd been in the hospital down in Perth before he'd been sent to jail.

Maddie touched her mother's forehead and then stepped

backwards. The pink froth was such an ugly colour. She'd never be able to eat fairy floss again. She took another step backwards. Her father was vomiting and his lips resembled glossy eggplants. No, she said, and shivered. No. A noise came out of her mouth and she ran forward and kicked the snake's head off her father's arm. He still did not look up at her, even as she began to kick at his legs and belly and the soft space between his legs. He didn't look up as she beat his head with her bare hands and pushed him over onto his back. The sisters, the two of them, just watched. The neighbours, when they arrived, found her in a gum tree, singing 'God Save the Queen'. Loudly. Porky said in court that he'd turned to kill a snake as his family was digging the vegie patch and in turning, his freshly sharpened shovel had caught his wife in the side of the head. He said a lot of things. It was only his two sane daughters who remained silent.

Acknowledgements

Everyone says that collections of short stories can't be published unless you are God. Or Alice Munro. Or both. Apparently, no one wants to read short fiction anymore. I think this is a sad and sorry state of affairs, since that effectively means I am no one. What does everyone else read in the bathtub when they don't want to risk their Fancy Pants novels to a puddle of warm water? What do they read when they are in the bathroom for (ahem) other purposes? Don't give me that hooey about *Reader's Digest* and crossword toilet paper.

Frankly, I like being someone instead of no one, and so should you. Preferably someone with a charming and delightful editor, like Georgia Richter (I have such a crush on that woman); eight charming and delightful children who laugh at my jokes and only roll their eyes sometimes (love them like crazy cakes); and charming and delightful Famous People like Debra Spark and C.J. Hribal and Ray Daniels and Bruce Aaron who read my work and help me fix it up so I don't look bad (I'll pay you guys when I get the royalty cheque or find some change in a pay phone, whichever is greater).

I'm gonna say this once and one time only: I love short stories. I love writing them and I love reading them. I want to take Fremantle Press out behind the water tank and kiss them passionately for publishing this, an untrendy, supposedly unmarketable book of short stories. You guys are my heroes in the publishing world.

Ultimately, this is a book about folks not finding love, not loving themselves, or not being able to give love. There's been a lot of that going around lately. Read the headlines: ick. It might have to do with reading *Reader's Digest* in the bathroom instead of short stories. I want to acknowledge, gratefully, the presence of the many people in my life who have taught me about love.

The following stories have appeared elsewhere: 'The Road to Katherine' in *StoryQuarterly*, 2007, and *The Kid on the Karaoke Stage & Other Stories* (Fremantle Press, 2011); 'You Lose These' in the anthology *Keep Your Wives Away From Them* (North Atlantic Books, 2010); 'Everything You Always Wanted to Know' in *Windy City Queer* (University of Wisconsin Press, 2011); 'The Telephone of the Dead' in *Prairie Schooner*, 2010. 'The Telephone of the Dead' was a finalist in *Glimmer Train*'s 2009 short fiction competition.

Langston Hughes' poem 'Mother to Son' in 'C.H.A.R.M.I.N.G.' at p. 128 is reprinted by permission of Harold Ober Associates Incorporated. The quote in 'Everything You Always Wanted to Know' at pp. 209–10 is from Dr David Reuben, *Everything You Always Wanted to Know About Sex (But Were Afraid to Ask)* (McKay, 1969), p. 132.

Also available from Fremantle Press

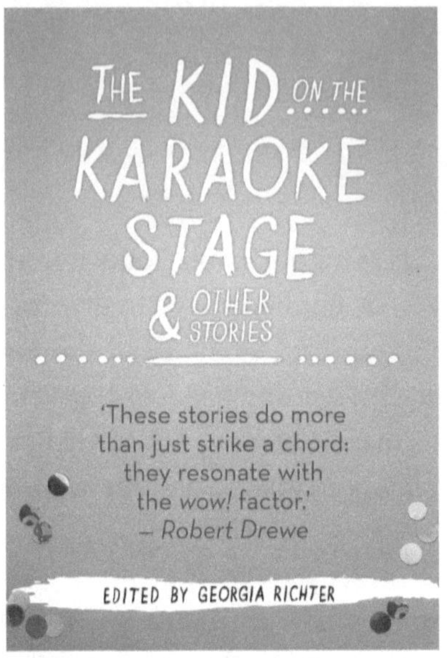

Twenty-eight life-changing stories about who we are, and what we want to be.

Edited by Georgia Richter. Featuring writing from Amanda Curtin, Jon Doust, Peter Docker, Goldie Goldbloom, Alice Nelson and many more.

This whole collection is brimming with vibrant and original writing – Brenda Walker

Also available from Fremantle Press

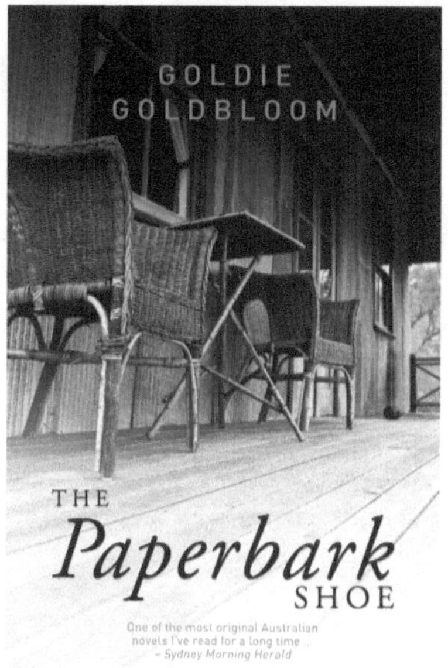

Winner of the US Association of Writers and Writing Programs' (AWP) Novel Award.

Winner of the Great Lakes Colleges Association (GLCA) New Writers Award.

Sydney Morning Herald *Pick of the Week*

... an assured debut written in beautifully precise language
– The Age

... a haunting tale of extreme hardship ... startlingly provocative ... it is impossible not to be touched by her characters
– The West Australian

First published 2011 by
FREMANTLE PRESS
25 Quarry Street, Fremantle 6160
(PO Box 158, North Fremantle 6159)
Western Australia
www.fremantlepress.com.au

Copyright © Goldie Goldbloom 2011
The moral rights of the author have been asserted.

This book is copyright. Apart from any fair dealing for the purpose of private study, research, criticism or review, as permitted under the Copyright Act, no part may be reproduced by any process without written permission. Enquiries should be made to the publisher.

Consultant editor Georgia Richter
Cover designer Tracey Gibbs
Cover image photographer/copyright unknown

A catalogue record for this book is available from the National Library of Australia

ISBN 9781921696879 (paperback)
ISBN 9781921696893 (ebook)

Fremantle Press is supported by the Western Australian State Government through the Department of Cultural Industries, Tourism and Sport.

Publication of this title was assisted by the Commonwealth Government through Creative Australia, its arts funding and advisory body.

Fremantle Press respectfully acknowledges the Whadjuk people of the Noongar nation as the Traditional Owners and Custodians of the land where we work in Walyalup.

www.ingramcontent.com/pod-product-compliance
Lightning Source LLC
LaVergne TN
LVHW091130080826
845145LV00008B/2100

* 9 7 8 1 9 2 1 6 9 6 8 7 9 *